Dear STX,

Look, I can't let it end like this. When I think about not being able to talk to you, I feel like I'm losing my best friend. So I am going to tell you who I am.

My name is Katie McNamara. I live at 357 North Abbington Street, and my phone number is 555-1663. If you don't feel like telling me who you are, you can still write to me or call me. Honestly, I just want to be able to talk to you every once in a while.

Well, the big mystery is over. Now you can do whatever you want. I'll be waiting to hear from you.

Your loving friend,
Katie

Quickly I sent the letter into the computer before I had a chance to change my mind. But I knew I was doing the right thing. I wanted STX to know who I was. I would worry about the consequences later.

Programmed for Love

Marion Crane

BANTAM BOOKS
TORONTO • NEW YORK • LONDON • SYDNEY • AUCKLAND

RL 5, IL age 11 and up

PROGRAMMED FOR LOVE
A Bantam Book / July 1985
Reprinted 1986

Sweet Dreams and its associated logo are trademarks of Bantam Books, Inc. Registered in U.S. Patent and Trademark Office and elsewhere.

Cover photo by Pat Hill

ISBN 0-553-24824-3

Published simultaneously in the United States and Canada

Bantam Books are published by Bantam Books, Inc. Its trademark, consisting of the words "Bantam Books" and the portrayal of a rooster, is registered in U.S. Patent and Trademark Office and in other countries. Marca Registrada. Bantam Books, Inc., 666 Fifth Avenue, New York, New York 10103.

Printed and bound in Great Britain by Hunt Barnard Printing Ltd.

O   0 9 8 7 6 5 4 3 2 1

Chapter One

It's hard to believe that your whole life can get turned around in just one semester, but it can. Believe me. I am living proof. I was crazy about Bobby for a long time before that, but last term was when things started moving.

To start off with, you should probably know that Bobby Allen is just about the most beautiful human who ever walked the earth. He's very tall, with blond, wavy hair that usually falls down over one eye. His eyes are deep blue and sensitive. He's in great shape, too, because he's a wide receiver for the Washington High football squad.

Although I had been to all the games and seen him play, the first time I *really* noticed him was at a pep rally last year, our sophomore year, when he received an award for outstanding new player. Coach Steeby made a long speech about how Bobby wasn't just the best wide receiver he'd ever coached, he was the best he'd ever seen. He said Bobby could catch a cornflake in a snowstorm. We had all laughed at that. Bobby just stood in front of us, smiling down at his feet. He was nudging his left heel against his right toe, and he looked uncomfortable in his suit coat and tie. Bobby is definitely a T-shirt and jeans sort of guy.

He isn't just beautiful on the outside, either. A lot of the jocks are stuck-up and hang out only with the most popular kids. Not Bobby. He's nice to everyone. As you can see, I am really crazy about the boy. He's a one-of-a-kind person.

I, on the other hand, am pretty average. I'm not a star athlete, or number-one student, or most popular girl.

I come from a run-of-the-mill American family. I love my parents, and I guess I even love my little brother Charles, even though he's creepy most of the time. I guess I'm sort of pretty. I have short brown hair and light brown eyes. Actually, my eyes seem to change color, like when I'm out in the sun a lot. They can get almost green.

Theresa, my best friend, says they're my best feature.

The first time I actually talked to Bobby was in the middle of last term, about the beginning of November. I was running, to make it to my ten o'clock class before the bell. As I was rounding the corner of B wing, I knew, if I really pushed it, I could make it on time. Then, wham! I ran smack into someone coming around the corner from the other way. The next thing I knew, I was sitting down with my books scattered all over the hall and I heard the last bell. Frantically I began to pick up my books.

I wasn't even thinking about whom I'd run into, when a soft, warm voice said to me, "I'm such a jerk. Here, let me give you a hand." I looked right up into Bobby Allen's blue eyes, and I thought I would dry up and die right there.

"Oh, it's OK," I said to him. "It was my fault. I should have been watching where I was going."

"No, it's my fault. Here," he said, smiling, and handed me a stack of books. "You're Katie, right?"

I couldn't believe he knew my name! I stammered something that I hoped sounded like yes.

"I'm Bobby Allen."

No kidding, I thought, but I just said, "Hi."

Bobby looked at me kind of funny. "Do you always wear just one earring?"

"What?" I asked, feeling my ears. Sure enough, one of my earrings was missing. "Oh, no," I moaned unhappily. "Mom gave me those garnets for my sixteenth birthday."

"Don't worry," Bobby said as he glanced around the floor. "Wait a minute, here it is." He reached down and handed me the lost earring. It had been right at my feet.

"Thanks," I said.

"Where were you going in such a hurry?" he asked.

"I've got that new computer class with Miss McIntyre. They finally got all the equipment installed, so the class is new in the second half of the semester."

"I know. I've got her class this afternoon," he said. He turned and started walking with me toward the room.

"I wonder what it's like," I said.

"I don't know, but she's supposed to be very nice," he answered.

I didn't care any more how late I was to class, but I was disappointed that because everyone else was in class, there was no one to see us walking down the hall together. I was sure that that would be the last time we'd ever be alone together, and I wanted a little recognition. We stopped at the door, and there was one of those awkward moments where neither of us knew what to say next. After a second Bobby stepped back, gave me a wave, and said, "Maybe I'll see you."

That's when I did something really dumb. See, I have this way of saying yup all the time. I started to say it, and then I decided to say sure, which might have sounded more relaxed, but somewhere in the middle my mouth and brain got all mixed up. I gave Bobby Allen my brightest smile and said—"Shup."

Bobby gave me a funny little smile, and I was certain I saw the words, "not a brain in her head," flash across those beautiful blue eyes. "Bye," he said as he turned to leave. I went into my computer class and managed to sneak in without making too much noise. Theresa had saved a seat for me next to her.

Theresa Moore and I sit together in all the classes we share, something we've done for most of our lives. Theresa has a very exotic, dark kind of beauty. I just love the way she looks. Her hair is cut short on the sides, but long in the back. Her eyes are dark brown, and she always wears the greatest clothes. But the best thing about her is that she's always there when I need her.

She knows me better than anybody, and she always knows what to do to help me when my life is lying in pieces around my feet.

So when I sat down next to her in computer class that day, I immediately whispered the whole story of what had happened with Bobby. And I couldn't believe it when she turned to me and started giggling. "Theresa, stop laughing!" I said to her. "It isn't funny. My whole life is practically ruined."

I think she even had tears in her eyes, she was laughing so hard. "Katie, it's no big deal."

"I said 'shup' to Bobby Allen."

"So?" She giggled.

"So! So, he probably thinks I have a speech impediment or that I'm just plain loony or something. I wish I were dead."

"Don't worry so much." Theresa tried to comfort me. "Bobby probably wasn't even listening."

"Thanks a lot. That makes me feel much better."

"Shh, Miss McIntyre's looking this way."

We shut up quickly, and I took my first careful look around the classroom. Actually, it was really interesting. All of the computer equipment was new. Each student was sitting at a small desk that was enclosed on two sides by low soundproof panels. In front of each of us was a computer keyboard and a small television screen. At the front of the room was a big chart with a picture of a keyboard, just like the ones on the desks. The room really made me feel a part of the technological age. I turned my attention to Miss McIntyre. "Computers are just tools," she was saying. "They shouldn't be scary at all. After you get to know them, you'll find they can make your lives a lot easier."

Theresa began to giggle. "Shup."

"Did you say something?" Miss McIntyre asked Theresa.

"No, Miss McIntyre, I sneezed," she answered.

"Have a tissue," Miss McIntyre said, walking over to her and handing Theresa a box.

"Thank you," Theresa answered, turning beet red.

I gave a Theresa a kick under the table, and Miss McIntyre went on. "The best way I know to get you to work with the computers comfortably is to have you communicate with them as you would with one another." She pulled out a large stack of envelopes from the drawer of her desk.

"I put all your names into the computer and had it pair you up randomly with students from my other classes. At first, I used your names. Then I decided it might be more fun if you were all anonymous, so now you each have a number.

Please don't broadcast either your number or your computer pal's. At the beginning of each week, I want you to write a letter to your pal, who will be in one of my later classes. It doesn't have to be long. Just tell a little bit about yourself, how your day is going, things like that. Mainly, I want you to become familiar with the machine."

Using the big chart at the front of the room, Miss McIntyre explained how to enter our letters and to call the response letters up. I guess because I'm sort of a whiz in typing, the whole thing looked pretty simple.

After a quick demonstration, Miss McIntyre distributed our numbers. She walked around the room, dropping an envelope on each desk.

I opened mine and read the small slip of computer paper inside. It said my number was GHS5915 and my pal's was STX1150.

Theresa leaned over to me. "My number is TTK3227. Sounds romantic, doesn't it?"

"Theresa! You're not supposed to tell anyone your number. Anyhow, don't talk to me about romance."

"Come on, Katie," Theresa said. "Bobby will notice you. It just takes time."

"I haven't got any time," I replied. "Not when Tammy Sawyer is still around."

I looked across the room at Tammy. She and

Bobby had been quite an item for the last couple of months, but now rumor had it that it was all over. I couldn't believe it! Tammy is this Brooke Shields look-alike that every guy in school wanted to date. But the story was that Bobby had broken it off, not Tammy. Of course, she wasn't talking.

Theresa nodded her head toward Tammy. "Don't worry about her. This isn't a Miss America contest, you know."

"Theresa, all of life is a Miss America contest. And between Tammy and me, who do you think is going to win?"

Theresa thought for a second. "I'd vote for you for Miss Congeniality."

"Thanks a bunch." I sighed.

I was glad Bobby wasn't in this class, because if he were, he'd probably have to be nice to Tammy even though he wasn't dating her anymore. And I just wouldn't have been able to bear to see them together.

I never could understand what Bobby saw in Tammy. She is just about the most two-faced person I've ever known. Of course, the fact that each of those two faces is stunningly beautiful might have carried some weight with Bobby. After all, he's only human, and he *is* a guy.

Miss McIntyre had gone up the aisle giving out

the rest of the envelopes. Theresa turned to me again. "Well, at least Bobby knows your name, and he talked to you. I think that's something."

"Yeah, first I practically crippled him, then I lost my earring and my books and everything, and then I said 'shup' to him like a nerd. Right, that's a great start. Anyway, I'm not so sure everything's over between him and Tammy. They were at the Cottage together last Friday."

"They were with a whole bunch of other kids," Theresa said.

"Well, I don't know."

Theresa has the habit of scratching her head when she's tired of going over the same thing again and again. She was doing that now. "Look, Katie, you like him, don't you?"

"You know I do."

"Well, he's free and you're free, so what's the problem?" she asked.

"The problem is, he doesn't even know that I exist," I answered.

"That's not true," she snapped at me.

"It is," I snapped back.

"Are you girls having trouble figuring out the exercise?" Both of us looked up. Miss McIntyre was standing near our desks. All the other kids were either typing at their terminals or staring at us.

I turned bright red. "No, Miss McIntyre. We were just—"

She frowned a little. "Well, get to it then."

"Yes, Miss McIntyre," I said. Both Theresa and I turned to face the little TV screens, and I began to type my first letter to STX1150.

At first I didn't know what to say. I mean, I'm not the kind of person who can just walk up to anybody and introduce myself. So you can imagine I wasn't wild about writing a letter to someone I didn't even know.

But when I thought about it, I realized that whoever it was would never know who I was, so it wouldn't really matter what I said. This was a chance to get to understand someone, not just the stuff you usually know about people, like how they dress, what kind of foods they like, or who they want to go out with. It was a chance that wouldn't come along every day.

Like I said, I'm a whiz at typing, so it took me only a minute to get this on to the keyboard.

GHS5915 to STX1150
Dear STX1150,

Hi. I like your name. Can I call you STX for short? When we first got this assignment, I thought it was sort of stupid. You probably did, too. But I've been thinking about it. For me, there are a lot of things I'd like to talk to someone about, but I don't because they are just too private. Is that true for you, too? I bet it is.

So, why couldn't we be secret friends? You don't know who I am, and I don't know who you are, and we never have to. I don't have a lot of friends, just one real good one, but I've found that everyone can be pretty nice once you get to know them. What do you think? I think it's important that we promise not to tell anyone else the things we tell each other. And we shouldn't try to figure out who we are. Do you agree? Let me know in your letter if you do.

Sincerely,
GHS5915

I reread the letter quickly and checked the spelling. Then I did as Miss McIntyre had shown us, and I typed in "Save." Line by line, the letter disappeared into the computer. It was done. But maybe it wasn't such a good idea, I thought, suddenly terrified.

My letter had sounded, sort of, I don't know, a little too friendly. Had I opened myself up to the wrong person? I didn't want my computer pal to get the wrong idea. Maybe I should have thought it out better. But how could I get the letter back after it had gone into the system?

"Miss McIntyre?" I called.

"Yes, Katie?" She walked over to my desk.

"Once we've entered our letters into the computer, uh, when do our pals get them?"

"Next Monday everyone will read their letters from their pals."

"Yes, but—"

"Just a second, Katie," she said, cutting me off. She walked off to help someone else, leaving me with my mouth hanging open.

"What's wrong?" Theresa asked. "You look like you just stepped on a cat."

"Nothing. Nothing is wrong," I muttered.

Theresa pretended to punch the keyboard. "I haven't even gotten a letter from my pal, and already I hate this. I don't know what to say. What'd you say in yours?"

"What?" I didn't know if I should tell her or not.

"What is wrong with you, Katie? I asked you what you wrote in your letter."

"Oh, nothing. Just stuff." I hated lying to Theresa.

Theresa went back to her letter. "That's a lot of help."

I raised my hand to ask Miss McIntyre how to recall the letter, but just then the bell rang.

"There! Finished just in time," Theresa said as she entered her letter. "Hey, look! Isn't it neat how this works?"

"Yeah. Neat." I thought about the whole deal while Theresa was getting her books together. It really wasn't that bad. I mean, the worst thing that could happen would be if my pal wrote back saying it was a really stupid idea. Probably all he or she would say was, "No, thanks." Still, I had the feeling that no matter how stupid it sounded, it was the right thing to do.

Theresa picked up her bag and stood up. "What's your number?" she asked.

"The one I got or my own number?"

"Your pal's number," she said.

I got my stuff together and started out the door. "STX1150."

Theresa smiled. "I bet it's a guy."

"Oh, come on, Theresa. Why do you think it's a guy?"

She pushed a little ahead of me, and we broke into the river of people crowding its way to other classes. "Just intuition."

We walked a little further without saying much. That's what's so nice about Theresa and me. We're good enough friends that we don't

14

have to talk or entertain each other all the time. Sometimes she knows what I'm thinking about before I do.

"Bobby's neat," she murmured. "You know, I think you two are perfect for each other."

"Someone should tell him." I laughed in spite of myself.

Theresa smiled. "Maybe I will."

I stopped and grabbed her arm, spinning her around. "If you do, Theresa, I will never, ever speak to you again!"

"OK, OK," she said. "I was just kidding."

I went on walking. "I really care about Bobby, and I don't want him to think I'm just some starry-eyed girl."

And then, wouldn't you know it, I spotted Bobby coming down the hall.

"There he is," Theresa whispered, noticing him at the same time I did. She nudged me in the ribs. I was sure Bobby noticed. I didn't think he was going to look at me, but then our eyes met, and he broke into a big grin. He held up his arms as if he were blocking on the football field. "Hi. How was the computer class?" I couldn't believe he was talking to me as though he were really interested in me. But, as I told you, that's Bobby.

"Fine," I said. I pointed to his arms, which

were still in the blocking position. "What's that for?"

"Just protection. You can really knock a guy over when you're moving." He jogged a little back and forth. Theresa burst out laughing. Bobby put down his hands and joined us. "I only hope Miller Central's line is a little easier on me tonight."

In spite of being compared to a whole football team, I had to laugh, too. "You know my friend, Theresa, don't you?"

"Sure." Bobby smiled. "I used to cut your dad's lawn."

Theresa looked as if she were going to fall through the floor. "Oh, no. I was hoping you wouldn't remember that."

Bobby laughed. I love his laugh. He just throws his head back and lets loose. "Yeah, I remember. I was just a kid. He stopped using me because I ran over the hose one day. Cut it to bits."

"Oh, well, my dad can be a drag sometimes," she said to him.

"No, he was right. I was just too young to be doing that sort of thing," Bobby answered. "Well, I've got to run. Hope I'll see you later." Before either of us could answer, he was halfway down the hall. Theresa and I just stood there looking after him.

I finally found my voice. "You know, he is just too beautiful. Every time I talk to him I'm not sure if he's real." Theresa still hadn't said anything. I nudged her. "You know what I mean?"

She turned to me slowly. "Shup."

Chapter Two

Just seeing Bobby put me in a better mood. But I should have known it couldn't last. Theresa and I made our way down the line of green lockers in the hall to good old number 249. That's mine. I am sure it's the worst one in the school. It never opens unless I dig my finger in this little hole, which is all sharp around the edges, and pull up. Then, the stupid thing won't close unless I slam it as hard as I can.

"I positively hate this locker!" I yelled.

Theresa's is right next to mine. Of course, hers opens with effortless grace. "Why don't you report it? If you report it, they'll come and fix it right away."

"I have reported it," I lied. "Three times. Theresa, let me use a pen."

"You're not going to ruin another one of my pens, Katie," she said.

"I won't ruin it. I just need to stick it in that little hole. Come on, Theresa. I've only got a pencil, and I don't want to cut my finger."

"No," she said flatly.

"Please?"

"Katie, you've already broken three of my pens. This is the only one I've got, and it's my favorite."

"I promise I won't break your pen, Theresa."

Theresa looked at me as if I were asking her to give up her firstborn child or something. Then she handed me the pen. "Here. But be careful," she warned.

"I will." I dug the pen into the little hole and started to feel for the latch.

Theresa closed her locker and leaned against it. "So, what's your battle plan?"

"What are you talking about?" I asked her.

"The beautiful Bobby Allen. What are you going to do next?"

I dug around with the pen. Sometimes it's really hard to find that stupid latch. "Theresa, you make it sound as if I have to trap him or something," I said.

"Don't be stupid, Katie. You do have to trap him. He's a guy, isn't he? Do you really expect him to come up with the idea on his own?"

"It'd be nice." I smiled.

"You'll get old and die waiting for that."

I stopped trying to open the locker for a second and turned to Theresa. "I told you: Bobby's special. I am not going to figure out a whole bunch of dumb schemes to get him to fall for me." Once again I started to work on the locker.

"Why not?" Theresa had her eyes glued on her pen.

"Why not? Because it just isn't right, that's why not."

All of a sudden I smelled heavy, expensive perfume, and I saw Theresa tensing up. I looked over my shoulder and there, in all her made-up glory, was Tammy Sawyer. "Hi, Katie. Theresa," she said coolly.

"Hi, Tammy," I answered. Theresa didn't even say hello. She doesn't put up with people she doesn't like.

Tammy just stood there staring at us. Well, actually she was staring at me. With her long, dark hair and piercing green eyes, she looked as if she'd just stepped off the cover of *Cosmopolitan*. There wasn't a hair out of place. I swear I've never seen her wear anything twice. She had on

Calvin Klein jeans—skintight, of course—a pair of red, spike heels and a long blue sweater. Even I would have stared at her if she was walking down the street.

She didn't go on with the conversation, so I figured I should say something. "Did you like the computer class?"

"No." She said it as though I'd just asked her if she liked having peanut butter jammed in her ears. "It's so cold in there, I thought I was going to die. And I think typing is terrible."

"What a tragedy," Theresa drawled.

Tammy didn't seem to notice. "Listen, sweetie"—I hate it when people call me sweetie, it's so condescending—"I hear you've got your eye on Bobby."

"Who told you that?" I asked her.

"Never mind. I just heard. I only came by because I think you're nice and I'd hate to see you make a fool of yourself."

Theresa laughed. "Well, isn't that generous of you."

Tammy went right on. "Bobby's not interested in anybody but me, sweetie, so don't waste your time."

I found my voice. "That's not what I've heard. I've heard Bobby's a free agent, *sweetie.*"

Tammy lost just a beat on that, then she

smiled sweetly. "Well, believe me, it is only temporary. He'll come to his senses."

"I think he already has," I said. I knew I was being rude, but it took everything I had to be even that polite.

"Well, don't say I didn't warn you. Bobby's just a little boy at heart, and I know what a little boy likes." She smiled.

"So do I, Tammy." I shouldn't have gotten as mad as I did, but I couldn't help it. "Little boys like collecting snakes and spiders, and I think Bobby's outgrown that. Maybe that's why you're not seeing so much of him lately."

Tammy glared at me openmouthed. Then she stalked off down the hall.

I turned to Theresa. "I shouldn't have said that. I think I really hurt her feelings."

"That's pretty strange," Theresa said. "I mean, why is she getting so upset? You only talked to him."

"That *is* strange," I agreed.

"Something's up, Katie," Theresa went on. "She wouldn't be acting like that if she didn't know something."

"Know what?" I asked. "There's nothing to know. Nothing is going on. That's the whole problem."

"See, that's why you need a plan," Theresa insisted. "You can bet she's got one."

"I told you, Theresa, I am not going to pull any stuff like that. If Bobby likes me, he likes me, and that's that," I said confidently.

"OK. But I think you're being stupid," Theresa answered.

My locker finally opened with a snap. The snap was Theresa's favorite pen cracking in two.

"My pen! You broke my pen!" she cried.

"Oh, come on, Theresa." I reached into my locker and pulled out one of my new pens. "Here, you can have this one."

"This one has blue ink. Mine had purple. It isn't the same thing."

I grabbed the books I needed and gave Theresa another pen. "Here, this one's red. Just use them both at the same time. We're late." We ran off together to study hall.

After school a lot of the kids like to go to the Cottage. It's a funny little hamburger place, sort of dumpy, but the food is good, and it's cheap, and they don't care if you make a lot of noise. The booths are covered in torn and taped vinyl, and the chairs are hazardous because they're not too sturdy. But the jukebox is good.

Theresa and I met there that afternoon. All the

booths were taken, so we sat at a table, Theresa ordered Cottage fries; I had a Tab. "Maybe you ought to find out if Bobby's having trouble with any of his classes and then offer to tutor him," she said.

"Theresa!" I moaned.

"OK. I'm just trying to help," she mumbled through a mouthful of fries.

"Besides, everyone knows Bobby's really smart. Straight A's."

"Maybe you could get him to tutor *you*," she offered.

"Oh, please."

"Hey, speak of the devil," Theresa said, nodding toward the door.

I turned and saw Bobby walking in with Tim Rogers and some of the other guys from the football team. He saw me and waved, and I felt a little flutter in my heart. "He's just so nice," I murmured. I turned around to face Theresa again.

Theresa touched my hand and smiled. "Don't worry. Look, he's coming over."

"What?" I gasped. I tried not to turn around and check as Bobby walked up to our table.

"Hi. Can I sit with you guys?" he asked, smiling at us.

"Sure." I smiled back. He hung his jacket over the back of his chair, then sat down. His arm brushed against my shoulder, and I thought I was going to die. I tried to calm down and talk like a human being. "No practice today?"

"No, just a short pep talk for tonight's game." He called across the room. "Hey, Ida. Can I have a mocha fudge shake?"

"Sure thing, honey." Ida yelled. Ida is a waitress, and she's about a hundred years old, but you can tell she used to be beautiful. Theresa says her dad told her Ida was a waitress there when he was in high school.

"Coach says I've got to put on some weight." Bobby folded his hands in front of him. It might have been my imagination, but I thought he was talking more to me than to Theresa.

"I wish somebody'd tell me that." Theresa moaned. "If I look at a shake, I gain five pounds."

"Me, too," I said.

Bobby laughed. "How come every girl I know says she's got to diet? I think both of you look terrific."

"Thanks," I said.

"Are you coming to the game tonight?" he asked.

"Wouldn't miss it," I said. "I go to all of them."

"You do?" He seemed surprised, as though he thought football was the most boring thing in the world and he couldn't believe I was interested in it.

"Sure. My whole family goes. My father used to play football in college, at Western."

"Wait a minute. Your father isn't Paul McNamara is he?" Bobby asked.

"Yes, why?" I was stunned that he'd know my father's name.

"I've heard of him. He was all-state three years in a row. Coach Steeby says he could've played pro," he said excitedly.

"That's him." I nodded.

"Boy, that's something. Did he have a nickname?" he asked.

I laughed. "Yup, Shotgun. My mom calls him that sometimes."

Bobby smiled at me. Theresa offered Bobby some fries. He took a couple and had one in his mouth just as Ida brought him the shake. "Thanks, Ida," he mumbled.

"Don't talk with your mouth full, hotshot." Ida ripped off a check and set it down on the table. "You want anything else here? I'm going on break."

Bobby looked right at me. "You want anything?"

At that moment I would have killed for a

mocha fudge shake with extra whipped cream like the one in front of Bobby.

"No, thanks," I said.

"OK." Ida said as she walked away.

"Have you always liked football, Bobby?" Theresa asked.

Bobby took a sip of the shake. "Yeah, it's because of my dad."

I realized I didn't know anything about Bobby's family. "Did he play?"

"No, he was born with a bad leg, and he's kind of short, but he always loved the sport. We used to watch games together even when I was just a baby. I was really glad it turned out I had a talent for it. It was like doing something for him. He's a great guy."

"That's terrific," I said. Bobby just got better and better.

Just then Tim stood up and yelled for Bobby to come over to his table.

Bobby stood up and picked up his shake. "I've got to go. We want to discuss some strategies for the game. See you tonight?"

"You bet," I said. He turned and waved again as he walked off.

Theresa stood up. "I've got to get going, too, Katie."

I checked my watch and saw that it was almost

four. "Darn, I do, too. I'm supposed to go running with Mom this afternoon." We paid our checks and headed for the door. Bobby was deep in conversation as we left, so I didn't say anything to him.

"Do you want a ride?" Theresa asked me once we were outside.

"No, thanks," I answered. "I feel like walking a little. I have a lot to think about."

"You sure do," Theresa said, giggling. "Pleasant daydreams." Then she hopped in her car and was off.

You know, I don't think I'd ever felt as strongly about anybody as I felt about Bobby. There had been other guys I thought I liked, but this was something different. Bobby was special, so different from all the other boys I knew.

As I walked toward my house, Bobby's image kept popping into my mind. His sensitive blue eyes beamed out at me, and he kept repeating, "See you tonight."

Chapter Three

"Come on, Katie, just one more mile," my mom said, urging me on. She and I jog three times a week, usually before dinner. We were up to five miles. It's nice because, besides the exercise, it gives us a chance to be alone. I know a lot of kids aren't wild about spending too much time with their parents, but I really like mine. Not just love, everybody loves their parents, but I really like mine.

My mom looks much younger than she is. In fact, people have mistaken us for sisters more than once. She has brown hair the same color as mine, but she wears hers shoulder length. Her eyes are blue, I've got my dad's eyes. She dresses really well, too. She's an architect, but she studied dancing for years, and she still has that funny ballet dancer's waddle.

Mom never treats me like a kid. As long as I'm not doing something totally off the wall, she's all for me. Even if it's not what she'd do herself. I guess that's why we get along so well. Of course, both she and my dad are still a little strict about certain things, like what time I have to be home at night. Dad, by the way, produces and directs television commercials. He has dark, curly hair, dark eyes, and a strong, compact body. He still looks like a football player.

As my mom and I went into our last mile, I gasped, "Slow down, Mom! We're not supposed to be racing."

"You were the one who set the pace, dear," she said, laughing.

"That was before I knew how tired I was." I thought I was about to die. She slowed down, then stopped and leaned against a tree. "Let's rest here for a second, and then we'll pour it on for that last mile." I dropped to the ground. I could hear the blood pounding in my ears.

Mom looked down at me and chuckled. "You lie down like that after running and you're never going to get up again."

"Right now, that sounds wonderful." She

made me get up and stretch a little. Then we just sat still for a minute. It was quiet and calming. I could hear the sound of our breathing. It was one of those moments that was just perfect for a mother-daughter chat.

I know a lot of kids feel funny asking their parents for advice, but I don't. Still, I didn't want to come right out and tell Mom about Bobby because she might have made the whole thing into a big deal. I figured it would be better to sort of slide into the issue. "Mom," I asked, "how did you get Dad to notice you?"

She sat back on her heels and laughed. "Well, it wasn't so much my getting him to notice me. Actually, I was fighting him off for a long time."

"No kidding?" I said.

"No kidding. He was probably the most popular guy in college at the time. Girls would fall all over themselves every time he walked down a hall. Well, I was an uppity, too-good-for-everybody architecture student. I guess after going away to dance school in Chicago when I was just fifteen, I felt more grown up than the other kids. I had an attitude problem."

"What sort of attitude problem?"

"Well, I was big stuff at dance school, so I felt special. But when I left dance, all of a sudden I was just a normal kid in a normal college. Believe me, I wasn't happy about it at all. In Chicago I'd only spent time with other dancers, even though we weren't really close. I didn't know how to make friends. And then your father came along. He was popular, good-looking, witty. I guess the truth is, he was everything I wanted to be at college. I was actually very shy around him."

I just sat there, silent. I couldn't believe my mom had ever been like that. "Wow," I said.

Mom looked at me and laughed. "What's the matter?"

"I just can't believe—I mean—"

"Yes, your mother wasn't always the perfectly beautiful, wonderful, kind person she is today." She laughed out loud.

"So, what happened?" I asked.

"Nothing happened. I kept avoiding your father, and we never got married, and you are just a figment of my imagination."

"Come on."

"OK. Well, your father, for some strange reason, started asking me out, and after about a hundred refusals, I finally said yes. I was so serious, but he soon forced me to laugh at myself."

I smiled. "That's so romantic."

"It is, isn't it?" she said wistfully. She reached over and fluffed my hair. "So, who's the guy?"

"What guy?" I'm not really good at playing innocent.

"What guy?" my mom asked, snorting. "Don't kid your poor old mother, Katie."

"Well, his name is Bobby," I admitted. "Bobby Allen. You don't know him."

"Is that Carl Allen's son?" she asked.

"I guess so. Yes." I answered.

My mom smiled. "Well, you've got good taste."

"You know who he is?" I felt a little embarrassed.

"I know his father." Mom stood up and started stretching. "His father's a great guy. We worked together on a charity drive last spring. Bobby's a star on the football squad, isn't he?"

"Uh-huh."

"I remember the last game we went to, your father talked a lot about him. He was very impressed."

That made me feel good. My dad isn't impressed easily.

"So, are you going out with him?" she asked me.

I pulled up some grass and started ripping the blades apart. "Not exactly." Mom didn't say anything. "I think he likes me," I went on. "I don't know. He talks to me, but I'm not sure if he likes me the way I like him. There's this other girl, too."

"Uh oh." Mom stopped stretching and paid full attention to me.

"Yeah. Well, supposedly they're not together anymore, but I'm not sure if that's true. Theresa says I ought to be scheming to get him to notice me, but I think that's kind of stupid. If he likes me, he'll let me know, and if not, there isn't much I can do about it. I don't know, though. Maybe I ought to start wearing makeup or doing something with my hair."

Mom put out her hands and helped me up. She was right about sitting down after running. I was pretty stiff. "I think you're beautiful, Katie. With your delicate skin, you don't need makeup, and your hair is lovely just the way it is."

"I'm your daughter. Would you tell me if I were a hopeless mess?"

"Probably not," she said, laughing.

"Thanks a bunch."

Mom hugged me. "Look," she said, cupping my chin with her hands. "I'm sure this Bobby is a nice guy. He must be if you like him. So you don't need to trap him into liking you. I think you've got the right idea. Do you think this other girl used schemes to get him interested?"

I thought about Tammy. "I'm sure of it."

"Well, maybe that's why they aren't seeing each other now. If you get people interested in you by pretending to be something other than what you are, you'd better be prepared to keep it up for a while. Because after they find out that the whole thing was just put on, well, it's sort of a lie, isn't it?"

"Yeah, you're right." Mom smiled at me. I smiled back. "How'd you get so smart so young?"

She laughed. "Oh, you are a sweetie. But I suppose you think, just because you're saying such nice things to me, that I'm going to let you beat me home."

"You aren't?"

She took off. "Not a chance," she called back to me.

Mom beat me home by a good quarter mile. We got showered and sat down at the table just as Dad was pulling dinner out of the oven.

We have kind of an unusual dinner arrangement. Because both my mom and dad work, we all take turns making dinner, even Charlie, who's only eight. We help him, of course. And we all take turns cleaning up, too. Most of the time it works pretty well.

Charlie was sitting in his chair wearing his Walkman, which is practically glued to his ears all the time. He had a Rolling Stones album turned up so loud even I could hear it. Mom frowned at him. "Walkman off at the table, Charlie."

"Whaaaat?" he yelled.

She picked up the Walkman and smiled at him. Then she pressed the talk button and yelled, "Walkman off at the table!"

Charlie whipped off the headphones. "OK! You don't have to make a person deaf!"

"If you keep your Walkman that loud all the time, you won't need Mom to do it for you," I said. I snitched a small bite of the chicken Dad had fixed. It was terrific. "Great dinner, Dad."

He'd made marinated chicken, pea pods, and broccoli, which he served over rice. It was delicious. When I was almost finished eating, I said, "Dad? Can I take off a little early for the game tonight? I want to catch a ride with Theresa."

"You've got dishes tonight, Katie," he said flatly.

"I know. I thought maybe you'd trade with me. I'll do them Sunday."

"I'll do them tonight if you'll do Sunday and next Friday," he offered with a grin.

"That's not fair. Two nights for one," I argued.

He smiled at me. "Nobody said life was fair, Katie."

"Can't Charlie do them?" I asked.

Charlie piped up, "I'm too little!"

Mom looked up at Charlie. "Why is it that whenever someone suggests you do some work around here you say you're too little and whenever I tell you you can't do something, you say you're grown-up?"

Charlie smiled at her. "I'm no dummy."

"OK, Katie. I'll trade tonight for Sunday," my dad finally said and laughed.

I jumped up and kissed him. "Great! Thanks, Daddy."

"But next time we play Monopoly, I get to be the ship," he added.

"OK." We shook hands on it.

My dad winked at my mom, and she smiled. They're really romantic together. It was hard for me to imagine that my mom had ever really avoided him.

"Hey, Dad, is it true that when you were in college, you had to practically beg Mom to go out with you?" I asked him.

Dad helped himself to more rice. "Not the way I remember it. You see, she was always following me around. I finally felt sorry for her and asked her out. She was sort of a skinny, ugly little thing—"

"Give me a break, Paul," Mom said, laughing.

"OK," Dad said. "She was the girl of my dreams. Beautiful, witty, rich. Rich was the best part. Her father used to pay me to take her out."

"Stop it!" Mom cried as Charlie and I giggled.

"Of course," Dad went on, "she did refuse my charms at first, but that was before she realized what a truly wonderful human being I was."

"I realized if I didn't go out with you, you were going to hound me for the rest of my life," Mom said.

I got up and took my plate to the sink. "Can I please be excused. Theresa will be here any minute, and I've still got to do my hair."

Dad grinned. "I like your hair like that. All wet and stringy."

I walked over to him and wrapped my arms around him. "No wonder Mom went out with you. You have so much charm."

He kissed me on the cheek. "So I've been told."

I pinched his nose hard enough for him to yell, and I ran out of the room.

I didn't think it would be scheming if I paid a little more attention to how I looked that night. I slipped on my new khaki pants and the white cotton shirt Theresa had given me for my birthday. I had to choose between being warm in my down jacket or looking good in my wool jacket. I picked the wool. I finished my hair just as I heard Theresa drive up. I pulled on my jacket, threw a scarf around my neck, and ran out to the car.

"Well," Theresa said to me, "don't we look spiffy."

"Why?" I asked. "Do I look overdressed?"

Theresa laughed. "No, you look terrific. But I think you're going to freeze in that wool coat."

I slammed the door. "Jeez, Theresa. Sometimes you sound like my mother. I am not going to freeze. It's not even that cold out."

Theresa gave me a knowing little smile as she pulled out of the driveway.

Chapter Four

We got to the game early and found great seats just behind the band. By kickoff time, my little wool coat and I were frozen solid. I don't think I've ever been so cold in my life. Theresa helped me thaw out by rubbing my arms a few times. Then the team ran onto the field, and she stopped. "Here they come!" she cried, pulling me to my feet. Bobby was right in front, number twelve. The band started playing the school fight song, and everybody was jumping up and down so hard, I thought the bleachers were going to shake to pieces.

I love going to football games. All those people bundled up, rosy-cheeked and excited. Everybody screaming and booing. The pom-pom girls cheering, and the band blasting.

The teams ran to the center of the field for the national anthem. Even though they were supposed to be standing still, I could see them bouncing and shifting on their feet. Who could blame them? Washington and Miller Central were old rivals, so this was one of the big games of the season.

By the second quarter, we were ahead fourteen to seven. Bobby had been playing wonderfully. It seemed he was everyplace at once. Then, just before halftime, as he jumped up to catch a high bomb, the guy who was guarding him hit him hard from behind. You could see it was a bad hit even before they crashed to the ground. The whole crowd came to its feet with one loud groan. We all watched in silent terror as Bobby limped off the field between two other players. Then the game started again without Bobby.

"Oh, Theresa!" I cried out.

"It's OK, Katie. Maybe he's not hurt that badly. This sort of thing happens all the time." Theresa was trying to reassure me, but the tone of her voice didn't sound very certain.

"I've got to see my dad," I said, and I jumped to my feet. I rushed down to the bleachers to where

I knew my family would be sitting. Dad looked serious. "Hi," I called.

Mom smiled up at me. "Hi."

"Dad, did you see Bobby get hit?" I asked him.

"Who could miss it?" He held out a small plastic cup, and my mom poured some hot coffee from a thermos into it. "I can't believe they didn't call clipping on that. The referee must be blind." The quarter ended, and the band came onto the field for the halftime show.

"Do you think he's hurt bad?" I asked.

"I don't know. They hit him pretty hard. It looked like a knee injury, which would cancel him for the rest of the game. But it could have been nothing. Possibly he just had the wind knocked out of him." Dad spoke in between sips of coffee.

My head was spinning at about a million miles an hour. Mom handed me a cookie. "I'm sure he's OK, honey." I smiled at her weakly and walked back to Theresa.

"Hey, Katie." She was standing with Pat Powers, who's the student manager for the team.

"Hi, Pat." I rushed over to him. "How's Bobby?"

He pushed his glasses up on his nose and grinned. "First Theresa drags me away from the hot dog stand and now you come dashing over, both asking about Bobby. Doesn't anybody care about how I am?"

Theresa punched him in the arm. "You didn't just have a Mack truck in a Miller Central uniform smash into you."

He laughed. "That's true."

"So, how is he?" I asked.

"Well, the coach is looking at him now. His knee got banged up a bit. He's fine, they just don't know if he should be in again tonight." He looked at me seriously. "I think I should tell you. He may never play the piano again."

"Bobby doesn't play the piano," Theresa said, trying to keep a straight face.

"He doesn't? Well, then it's no great loss." I like Pat a lot, but at that moment I could have hit him. Imagine, making bad jokes at a time like that!

"Look, Bobby's not hurt badly. He just may have to sit out the rest of this one game, but he's OK. I've got to go." Pat ran down the stairs toward the field. He turned at the bottom and yelled up. "I'll tell Bobby you were asking about him and that you both send him your best for a speedy recovery." He bowed from the waist and ran off.

"Do that!" Theresa yelled after him. She turned to me. "Well, what do you think?"

"I don't know. If it was anything serious, Pat would have been more upset, don't you think?"

"I guess so." We sat down, and I tried to concentrate on the halftime show. Finally, the teams came back out. Bobby wasn't on the field; Ted Dunn had replaced him.

Both teams scored right away, bringing the score to twenty-one to fourteen. We were still in the lead. Then, in the third quarter, Miller Central intercepted a pass and ran it back for a touchdown. With the extra point, the score was tied. We got stopped on our next advance, and Miller Central kicked in three points. There were only about three minutes left in the game when Coach Steeby called a time out. Miller Central was leading, twenty-four to twenty-one. People were beginning to leave, sure Washington would lose.

Theresa turned to me. "What do you think? Can we win it?"

"We have to." Somehow I didn't sound convinced. All of a sudden the whole stadium started cheering and yelling. "What happened, Theresa?" I said.

Theresa stood up on the seat so she could see better. "I don't know. It—look!" She pointed out to the field, and I saw Bobby running onto the field!

At that point, all our guys really began playing. But time was running out. We could only move the ball up an inch at a time because the Miller Central line had pulled together like a tight wedge on the forty-yard line. There were thirty seconds on the clock as Washington High lined up for the last play of the game. The center snapped the ball into the quarterback's hands, and we all held our breaths as he dropped back and let go of a high bomb. It seemed to take forever for the ball to come down, and when it did, it landed smack in the hands of glorious number twelve.

I know it's hard to believe, but for just a second there, the stadium was as quiet as a theater just before the curtain goes up. Then people began screaming as Bobby ran. Past the thirty-, the twenty-, the ten-yard line. Nobody even heard the gun go off. The game wasn't officially over until the last play was finished.

Bobby poured it on, clutching the ball to his side. He darted in and out of a horde of Miller Central monsters, all out to bury him. With a burst of speed, Bobby crossed into the end zone—six more points for us. Final score, twenty-seven to twenty-four, Washington High victorious.

People poured onto the field. Everyone was trying to get to Bobby to slap him on the back or give him a hug. I grabbed Theresa by the hand and pulled her with me into the crowd heading toward the field.

In the middle of that mass of people on the field was the team. Their once white-and-green uniforms were now grass- and mud-stained. Then two of the players lifted Bobby onto their shoulders. He rose triumphantly above the crowd and was carried toward the locker room. Cheering madly, the crowd followed him.

I pushed my way to the front of the group, and Bobby caught my eye. He smiled and yelled to me. "Hey! Hello!"

"Hello, yourself!" I yelled back. I'd long ago lost Theresa.

He flashed me this big grin. "So, what did you think?"

"It was a great game. How's your knee?" I yelled.

"It's nothing," he answered. The crowd started to pull him away, and I couldn't keep up. "Hey!" he yelled over his shoulder. "Are you going to be at the Cottage after?"

"Yeah." The crowd kept moving, and Bobby got farther and farther away.

"See you there," he yelled over their heads.

I stood still as the team disappeared into the

locker room. Suddenly, I felt someone grab my arm. It was Theresa. "What a game!" she said, out of breath from the excitement.

"Yeah," I answered in a daze.

"Where to now, Katie?" she asked me.

"The Cottage," I replied.

The Cottage looked only slightly more orderly than the scene on the field after the game. It was nothing but wild, screaming kids, drinking Cokes and eating burgers, everyone rehashing the last few minutes of the game. There was a big table set up in the center of the place for the team. Some of them were already there with their girlfriends and friends. Theresa and I joined two other girls we knew at a booth and ordered burgers.

We were there about twenty minutes before Bobby came in. He was in the center of a group that was yelling even louder than the crowd in the diner. People started chanting his name, and there was a mad scramble to clear a place for him at the big table. Of course, everyone on the team was getting a lot of attention, but the biggest fuss was made over Bobby. If it had been anybody else, he would have been milking it, but Bobby just looked tired and a little embarrassed. Mostly tired.

He glanced over and caught Theresa and me watching him. He smiled and waved us over. "Why don't you guys join us? There's plenty of room," he called.

There wasn't an inch of space at that table, but somehow chairs got shifted around, and we managed to squeeze in. I thought it might look a little pushy if I sat next to him, but Theresa started directing who was to sit where, and the only empty chair ended up right next to his. Like I said, Theresa's my best friend.

"What a game, huh?" exclaimed Ted Bobsey, one of our halfbacks.

"The best," answered Theresa.

Bobby just smiled at the soda in front of him. He was twisting the straw and staring at the table.

"How's your knee?" I asked. I didn't know what else to say.

"Oh, it's OK. It wasn't anything. I could have gone back in sooner, but Coach felt differently."

"Could have gone in sooner. Listen to him." Ted laughed and slapped Bobby on the back. "His knee was the size of a grapefruit."

"Well, it's a lucky thing he sent you back in, buddy," said Andy McCarger, another team member. "I couldn't believe that last play. I mean, when Pete let go of that pass, I thought it was way too short. I swear, Bobby, I think your fingers can grow at will."

"No," Bobby said, "Pete put that ball right into my hands. All I had to do was get down the field in time."

Ted laughed. "You also had to avoid about six hundred of those Miller Central guys. There was more action on that field than at the Giants game last night."

"Hey," said Andy, "what did you think of that game?"

Ted turned to Andy and launched into a long analysis of the Giants game. Bobby took a sip of his soda and looked at me, and suddenly it was as if we were alone. Sure, all those people were still around, but Bobby looked into my eyes, and for a second we were the only two people in the room.

I took the opportunity to start a conversation with him. "Was your father watching the game?" I asked.

Bobby smiled. "Yeah."

"I guess he was pretty happy."

"Yeah. I thought he was going to burst wide open, he was so excited after the game." Bobby smiled at me. "Pat told me you were pretty concerned about me when I got hit."

"Yeah," I said softly.

"Thanks. It means a lot when you're hurt to know people care about you, not just about the game."

"Well, it looked like you got hurt pretty badly. My dad said it was clipping."

"Maybe. I wasn't thinking about it much. Anyway, we won, and that's all that matters." He flashed that wonderful smile at me.

"I guess so." I smiled back.

As you can tell, I wasn't exactly making sparkling conversation. But at the same time, Bobby and I were finally having a real conversation, and it didn't seem forced at all. And I realized I was having a good time talking to him, as if he were another kid from school. Just another kid who happened to be the most beautiful, wonderful, kind, and caring boy on two feet.

We talked about school and our parents and stuff. It was so nice. There was a moment when we didn't say anything, and I thought Bobby wanted to ask me something. But just then the front door opened, and a gust of cold air blew in. With it came Tammy Sawyer. Her beautiful eyes zeroed in on our table, and she walked over. There was a chorus of hellos as she stepped up behind Bobby and put her hand on his shoulder.

"Hi, all." She smiled. "Hi, Bobby. Nice game."

Bobby looked up at her. "Thanks, Tam."

She held his eyes with hers for a moment, then a frown came over her face. "Bobby, honey, I am really in a fix."

"Why?" Bobby asked with concern.

"Well," she whined, "my car kept stalling on the way over here, and I'm afraid to drive it home. Could you drive me?"

I think all of the guys at the table were half out of their chairs hoping that Bobby would say no, but that just isn't Bobby.

He pulled his jacket off the back of his chair and got up. "See you all later."

Everyone started calling goodbye. Tammy turned and smiled right at me. "Good night, kids." Then she put her arm through Bobby's and they walked out.

Chapter Five

So much had happened over the weekend that I almost forgot about my computer friend. Most of the other kids had, too. But after Miss McIntyre reminded us on Monday to call up our letters, it all came back.

I got a little lump in my stomach as I sat at my desk. I waited for a minute, then realized the whole situation wasn't going to disappear just because I wished hard enough. So what was the worst thing that could happen? I could get a letter from a rude, insensitive person who would tell me my idea was stupid. So what? I'd never see him or her, anyway, and we could just finish out the semester writing dumb letters about nothing at all.

Oh, well, I thought, *I might as well get this over with now*. I tapped in my code and called up the letter. It fed onto the screen line by line.

STX1150 to GHS5915

Dear GHS,

Of course you can call me STX. Let me tell you, you sure know how to get right to the point. I wasn't expecting this assignment to be too hot. You know how teachers are always trying to get you into stuff like this, but it usually ends up being really dumb. Not with you as a computer pal.

Yes, it definitely bothers me, too, that people hide their feelings so much. I wasn't that aware of it until I got your letter. Then I started to think about how much time we spend in small talk. And that's sort of like building walls between people, isn't it? Sometimes it seems as if we're all so afraid of letting anybody get too close that we cover ourselves up with a lot of meaningless talk. I promise I'll try not to do that with you.

It's kind of hard to believe that you have

this problem, not opening up, I mean. From your letter you seem like a very open person. I wish I were more like that. I don't really have a lot of friends, either, although it would seem like I do. Not that I don't like all the people I hang around with because I do. But I'm not really close to any of them. I tried to get close to a person not too long ago, but it didn't work out. We just wanted different things. Getting close to someone is very hard.

Well, I guess I should finish this off. I promise not to try to figure out who you are, but maybe at the end of term we should talk about that again. I would hate to lose a good friend. Wouldn't you?

Best wishes,
STX1150

Boy, talk about a surprise! I was so excited about the letter that I answered it right away. I read STX's letter over again and organized my thoughts. It looked as though we were starting off terrifically, and I wanted my second letter to make STX feel as if we'd made the right decision. I typed in the heading and took off.

Dear STX,

What a wonderful letter! I had a lot of second thoughts about that letter I wrote you. I even thought about getting it back and changing it. Now, I'm really glad I didn't.

No, I don't really think of myself as an open person. In fact, I'm a little shy about talking to people in general and certain people in particular. I loved what you said about relationships being difficult. It's so true. It wouldn't be so bad if our errors didn't hurt so much.

I can't talk from experience because I've never really had a serious relationship with anybody. But right now, there *is* someone that I'm trying to get to know better. The problem isn't the other person as much as it is me. Every time we're alone I get all tongue-tied and can't think of anything to say. I just know that if we could really talk, everything would be OK. But I'm so afraid that this other person doesn't feel the same way, and that would just crush me. I don't know. Maybe, in a way, it would be a relief to know for sure one way or the other.

One thing that I'm proud of is that I am being as honest as I can with this other person. I don't want to pretend to be something I'm not just to get attention. I don't think that ever works, do you?

I'm sorry you had bad luck with your last relationship. Yes, it is hard knowing what you want out of a relationship with somebody.

Gosh, we've only exchanged two letters, and already I feel as if I've known you all my life. Funny, isn't it? I'm really looking forward to your next letter.

Yours truly,
GHS

As you can see, this whole thing was really beginning to develop into something. I know I'd decided to open up to STX, but I'd never expected to be this open. I mean, we'd only gotten through the first three letters, and I was already telling STX things I only said to Theresa.

It was funny, but that sort of bothered me. I felt as though I were betraying Theresa or something. She let me read her letters, and it was just what you'd expect, pretty normal stuff. I was very careful not to let her see either of mine or STX's. When she asked me about it, I just said that they were boring. I know that's not the way you should be with your best friend, but it was hard enough to get myself to understand what I was doing. There was no way I could explain it to someone else.

I knew STX understood, though. From the very first letter, STX caught on to what I was doing. As time went on STX would even say things that I already knew, but wasn't aware I knew. That was just what happened in the letter I got the next Monday.

STX1150 to GHS5915

Dear GHS,

How have you been? Sorry, that sounds a little like small talk. But that isn't the way I mean it. I've started to think more about little things like that. For instance, when people come up to me in the hall and say, "How are you?" do they really want to know how I am? I mean, how long would they hang around if I didn't say, "Fine, thanks?" So, now you know that if I ask you how you are, I really want to know.

You and I sure were lucky to get matched up. We really seem to be in the same place. Like, right now, I am also interested in this other person, but it looks like it's all one-sided. When I talk to this other person, she gets sort of distant, and I can't seem to get through to her. Also, there's another problem with another person, but I can't talk about that right now. Not even to you, GHS.

I don't understand why it's so hard to go up to somebody and let them know that you like them, that you want to get to know them better, but it is. If I could just talk to this other person the way I talk to you, everything would be OK. But I can't. In fact, I can't talk to anybody else this way, just you. I don't know if that's because we're faceless or if it's something else.

I definitely admire you for sticking to being honest with your other person. I don't know a lot about this, either, but I do know that a relationship that isn't based on honesty isn't a real relationship. It's nothing. So, stick to it. You're doing everything just the way it's supposed to be done. If it doesn't work out, well, I guess it wasn't ever meant to be in the first place. That may not be the most optimistic thought, but it's a comfort if things aren't turning out the way you want them to. So, my friend, stay just the way you are.

STX

Isn't that just the sweetest letter? That was when I first realized STX was a boy. He'd obviously tried to keep that hidden, but he'd messed up and let it slip that the person he liked was a girl. Then I started wondering if I'd ever messed up. Oh, well, it didn't really matter. We were too close already for that to change anything between us.

I was still curious about who STX was.

Sometimes I thought it was Pat Powers, who was in one of the afternoon classes. I couldn't say why—just an instinct. He had been standing at Theresa's locker one morning. When I walked up to them, he had given me a funny look. But he couldn't know if I was his partner or not, could he? Unless—I had told Theresa what STX's number was, and Theresa did talk to Pat a lot. If she'd let it drop . . .

Then I realized I was letting my thoughts get out of control. I didn't even know if Theresa had told Pat anything, and anyway, what if she had?

Why should I be so upset if STX discovered who I was? I wasn't ashamed of anything I'd told him.

Of course, if he was Pat and if he did know I was GHS, then he'd probably figured out that the other person I'd been talking about was Bobby. And then maybe he'd told Bobby. That's when I started wondering if my parents would be terribly upset if I quit school and moved to Peru!

Chapter Six

"How can you stand there and tell me you don't know what next month is?" Theresa cried excitedly.

"Theresa, I am not standing, I'm walking. Just get to the point," I answered.

Mom stopped to look in the window of a clothing store. She and Theresa and I had just finished lunch at the mall, where we had been all morning, and we were getting ready to do some more shopping. So far, I had tried on about fifty different pieces of clothing, all of which looked horrendous on me. I was beginning to suspect it wasn't the clothing's fault, so I wasn't in the greatest mood.

"Katie, do you know what size shirt Charlie wears?" Mom asked.

"What kind of a mom are you?" I snapped.

"The kind that can't remember a shirt size to save her life." Mom walked into the store, and we followed her. She's funny when she's shopping. As a successful architect, she has designed whole building complexes for big corporations; she has fourteen people working under her; and she's responsible for million-dollar projects. But in a department store, she can't make up her mind about a single thing.

We walked to the boys' section, and my mom began looking at shirts, "I don't think Charlie can wear a large in this," she said, holding one up.

"Get him a medium then," I offered.

"But the mediums all look so small," she replied.

"So get him a large, and if it's too big, he can grow into it." I was getting a little tired of all this.

"No, that won't work with Charlie. He'll wear it out long before that." She held the two shirts as if she were weighing them. See what I mean?

Theresa tugged at my arm. "I'm trying to help you, and you aren't even paying attention."

"Why? What do you think, the large or the medium?" I asked her.

"I'm not talking about that, you idiot! I am talking about next month," she cried.

"What's next month?" I asked.

"See what I mean?" She threw her hands up in the air.

Mom tugged at my other arm. "I think I'll get the large."

"Good," I said, sighing.

"Now, what color?"

"Oh, great." I could see the whole process starting all over again.

Theresa pulled at me once more. "Katie!"

"Theresa, you have to be patient right now. My mother needs me. She has chosen a size in record time, and now we're moving into color categories. After she decides that, I can talk to you."

"When will that be?"

"Come back next spring," I answered.

"Look, birdbrain," Theresa said and pulled me away from the counter where Mom was holding six different colored shirts up to the light, "next month is Christmas."

"So?" I said. "I've known that for weeks now."

"So, I have got a terrific idea. I'm going to have a party just before Christmas break."

"Great," I said.

"Yeah, great. I'm just going to invite a few

friends and some members of the football squad."

"Theresa!" I could almost see the little wheels in her brain turning. "Please don't cook up some ridiculous scheme."

"Come on, Katie, it's no big deal. I'm just going to have a Christmas party, and whatever happens after that is entirely up to you."

I watched some poor unfortunate salesgirl offer to help my mom. "Well, I guess it's all right. Yeah. In fact, Theresa, it's a wonderful idea."

"It is?" she asked, amazed that I'd changed my mind so quickly.

"It is!" All of a sudden the whole idea blossomed in my mind. A romantic Christmas party. What could be more natural? We wouldn't be scheming; we wouldn't be dishonest; and best of all, we wouldn't be inviting Tammy Sawyer!

"Well, I'm glad you're into it," Theresa said smugly, "because my mom already said it's OK. We'll just invite about twenty people. I don't want it to be too big."

"Yeah, twenty's about right," I agreed.

Mom had finally decided on a blue shirt for Charlie, and we went up to the counter with her to pay for it. Just next to the counter was a display with a whole bunch of accessories—you know, belts and things. Sitting right on top was a really great little bow tie. That's what gave me the idea.

"Theresa, why don't we make it formal?"

"Formal?"

"Yes! We could make the whole evening very—elegant. And very romantic. . . ." I let my voice trail off.

Excitement began to glow in Theresa's dark eyes. "What a great idea!"

Mom got her change, and we walked out of the store. "What's a great idea?"

"Theresa and I are going to throw a Christmas party at her house, and it's going to be formal."

Mom laughed. "Well, that'll be a change for most of your friends. No jeans?"

"Nope," we both said.

"I think it will be wonderful." Mom stopped. "Uh-oh."

"What's wrong?" I asked.

"Wait for me here a second. I forgot Charlie's shirt back in the store." She ran off back to the store, and Theresa and I sat down on a bench.

Theresa stuck a stick of gum in her mouth and began chewing wildly. She always does that when she's thinking. "OK, let's see. We'll have a lot of fresh flowers and candles and food and a punch bowl. Wait a minute!"

"What?"

"Oh, what an idea! We'll have a sit-down dinner!" she cried.

"What?" I wasn't quite sure what she meant.

"Just like in the movies. A big sit-down dinner with different courses and candles on the table and a centerpiece and—"

"Theresa, you can't do a sit-down dinner for twenty people."

Theresa looked dejected. "No. I guess not."

We both sat there for a second, and suddenly Theresa brightened up again. "I could do one for sixteen, though."

"Sixteen?"

"Yeah. That's how many my parents had for Thanksgiving. We've got all the plates and silverware." Theresa was hot now.

"What are your parents going to think?" I asked her.

"Oh, they'll love it. Anyway, it won't be that big a deal for them. We'll do all the cooking and the cleanup and everything. Isn't it just too much for words?"

The whole idea was beginning to sparkle and turn in my head. I could imagine it all. Everybody would be dressed in formal clothes, the table would be decorated with flowers and candles, and we'd have dancing afterward. On a night like that, anything could happen.

Still, I was a little concerned about Theresa asking Bobby. We'd talked an awful lot at school over the past few weeks, but I thought the incident between him and Tammy at the Cottage was a little strange. There was no reason he'd *had* to take her home. There had been a hundred guys there who would have been happy to do it, and I'm sure he knew it. There were only two reasons why he would have left—he was only being nice to her, or he really wanted to. Maybe everyone was right about them. Maybe they did really belong together and the breakup was only temporary.

"Theresa, what happens if you invite Bobby and he asks if he can bring Tammy?" I wondered out loud, suddenly worried.

Theresa gasped. "He isn't going to do that!"

"Well, what if he does?"

"We'll just say that there isn't enough food or something."

"Theresa, you can't say that!"

"Why not?"

"First of all, it sounds like a pretty lame excuse, and second of all, knowing Tammy, she'd probably say it was OK and bring a brown bag with her own food."

"Not Tammy. Never just a brown bag. It would have to be a Gucci or something."

"Theresa—"

"Look, Katie. He isn't going to say that. Get it through your head that it's over between them."

"It didn't look like it was so over at the Cottage that night after the game."

Theresa cracked her gum and sighed. "Well, it is. And I'll tell you something else. I think Bobby wants to ask you out and he would have that night if Tammy hadn't butted in."

"Then why hasn't he asked me?"

"Maybe you haven't encouraged him enough."

"Oh, come on."

Theresa threw her hands up in the air and turned her back on me. "Maybe it's because you said 'shup' to him that day in the hall," she said, teasing me.

I ignored the last comment. The truth was, he had spent most of his time talking to me, and after the game, he'd asked me specifically if I was going to the Cottage. But that didn't mean anything, did it? I mean, Bobby was always nice to everybody, and Theresa had practically pushed me into the chair next to his, so what choice did he have? But, I had gotten the feeling that he'd wanted to ask me something. . . .

This whole thing was too difficult. I made a mental note to talk to STX about it all. I'd found myself doing that a lot lately, making notes of things to ask STX. I'd think of something and I'd say to myself, *I should discuss that with STX.* In a lot of ways, I wished our relationship could be different. It would have been nice just to be able to call STX whenever I wanted to. But at the same time, STX was special to me because the time we spent together had limits, it had more—quality, I guess.

STX had said that if he could only sit down and talk to the girl he liked the way he talked to me, everything would be great. I felt exactly that way about Bobby. Well, it was worth a try. I tapped Theresa on the shoulder. "OK, the Christmas party is on, as long as *you* invite Bobby."

"All right!" Theresa laughed and cracked her gum. "Hey, where's your mom?"

Suddenly I realized she had been gone for quite a while. "Oh, that woman! She probably forgot all about us."

"Listen," Theresa said and stood up, "I've got to pick up some film for my camera, and the photo store is right next to that clothing place. I'll go get my film, and then try and find her. You wait here in case I miss her, OK?"

"OK."

Theresa walked off, and I just sat there, waiting. The mall wasn't very crowded for a Saturday, especially a pre-Christmas Saturday, but I did see several kids I knew. They each waved hello and went on. People use the mall like that. It isn't just a place to shop, it's also a place to meet or just hang out.

Then, just as I was getting ready to take off and try to find both Theresa and Mom, I saw Tammy. She was coming out of Ms. Style with a bunch of packages. I tried to look as if I hadn't seen her, but it was too late. She stared at me for a second and then came over to the bench.

"Hi," she said.

I felt a little funny because she didn't seem to be mad or anything. "Hi," I said.

"Mind if I sit down for a second? These packages are killing me." She put all her stuff on the floor and sat down next to me. She was smiling and being pretty casual. It was all very strange. "Are you just hanging out or shopping?" she asked me.

"Well, mostly shopping."

"Having any luck?"

"No, not much."

"I know the feeling." Tammy took a compact out of her bag and began fixing her already perfect face. "You should check out Ms. Style. They're having a terrific sale on a whole bunch of stuff. I got two great tops and a pair of jeans, all for almost nothing."

By this point I'd really begun to wonder what was going on. I had expected Tammy to bite me or something, and here she was talking as if we were best buddies. Like I said, strange.

"Hey, Katie." Tammy put her compact down and made her voice sound serious. "I know we're not exactly friends, and maybe I shouldn't have spoken to you the way I did that day at your locker." She stopped as if she expected me to answer her. But by now I was having trouble breathing. How could she expect me to do something complicated like put together a sentence?

Tammy went on. "The truth is, I've always thought you were pretty nice, even though I haven't spent much time hanging out with you. You know how it is, you only have time for just so many friends."

Gee, it must be tragic being so popular, I thought.

"I'm glad I saw you here because I've wanted to sit down with you and talk about my Bobby." She actually said *my* Bobby! "See, you might not know the whole story. Bobby and I did only go together for a few months, but we became very close. He's a different kind of guy than most, and you have to understand him. Sometimes he does things, and he doesn't think them out very clearly. You know what I mean?"

"No, I don't," I said frankly.

Tammy looked at me for a second. I thought I saw frustration in her eyes, as though her phony the-truth-is-I've-always-thought-you-were-pretty-nice routine was starting to crumble. Then she caught herself. "What I mean is, Bobby's just going through a phase, and it's nothing more than that. We are still very interested in each other."

I decided this had gone far enough. "Look, Tammy, I don't have the slightest idea why you're talking to me like this. I can't control what Bobby is feeling or thinking. It's true I am interested in him, but I think Bobby should be allowed to make up his own mind. You know, you sound as if I'm trying to kidnap him or something."

"It's just that you shouldn't be butting into things that you don't know anything about," Tammy said.

"Like what?"

"Like Bobby."

Tammy was starting to get really upset. Suddenly I realized something about her. Tammy may have been popular and beautiful, but she was not one bit sweet, and she knew it. Then I did something really mature. I smiled very sweetly and said, "I'm sorry if I'm upsetting you."

Tammy stood up and grabbed her packages. "You're not upsetting me, you're just making a fool out of yourself!" She screwed up all her dignity and tried to make a good exit. She might even have pulled it off if she hadn't dropped one of her packages and then two more while she was trying to pick up the first one. By the time she finally got away, all she needed were Larry and Curly and she would have been ready for a rerun of the *Three Stooges* show.

I had managed to stop laughing by the time Theresa and Mom got back, but I started again when I saw them.

"What happened?" Theresa asked. "How come you're laughing?"

"Yeah, what's so funny, Katie?" Mom asked.

I linked an arm through Theresa's and then Mom's and pulled them down the mall. "I'll tell you about it later. Right now, I need a romantic formal dress, and I hear Ms. Style is having a sale."

Chapter Seven

I made it to computer class on Monday morning right on time. Every teacher has a good idea once and a while. If Miss McIntyre had given us our letter-writing assignment to get us interested in computers, it was working like a charm. I couldn't wait to get to my terminal and talk to STX. That day I was even more interested in writing to STX than I was in getting his letter.

I began typing quickly, and when I finished, this was on the screen.

GHS5915 to STX1150

Dear STX,

Boy, has this been an incredible weekend!

Things have been wonderful one minute and truly awful the next. There were so many times I wished I could sit down and talk to you about what was going on in my head.

I feel so unsteady lately. When I look in the mirror, I'm not even sure it's really me I'm seeing. I don't think everybody is like this. I know there must be people who are always sure they're doing the right thing in every situation at every moment. I'm just not one of them.

This all has to do with my other person. My best friend thinks there is definitely something there, but I can't see it. Maybe that's because I can't really see what is so wonderful about me that anybody would fall for. I'm not saying that I'm a nerd or anything. It's just that this other person has so much going for him that I can't see what he'd see in me. If I were more sparkling or bright or beautiful or talented, then I could see it.

I know people who wake up beautiful in the morning, who have hair just the right shade to set off their perfect eyes, which are set in a perfect face made up of perfect skin which, heaven forbid, would never blemish.

So, that's my competition, and what's somebody like me supposed to do against that? I'm glad you think I'm doing the right thing by being honest. Believe me, it isn't easy. But it's easier knowing you approve. You've become like my conscience. I always wonder: what would STX think of this? Is that weird? Isn't that what a friend is really for? I think so. Sorry I've spent this whole letter talking about me.

Your friend,
GHS

I was eager to see how STX would answer, and I spent the whole week wondering. So you can imagine how I felt the next Monday when Miss McIntyre announced that we'd have to wait until the end of the period to do our letters. She had some computer problems for us to do first. I worked as fast as I possibly could and finished mine about twenty minutes ahead of the rest of the class. I brought my worksheet up to Miss McIntyre and set it on her desk.

"Having some trouble, Katie?" she asked as she looked up at me.

"No, I'm finished," I said, grinning.

She raised her eyebrows and smiled. "Finished?"

"Yes, ma'am."

"You know, Katie," she said and shuffled the papers in her hands, "I've noticed you have a definite flair for this. Your work has been excellent."

Hearing that from her made me feel great. As I said, she's a really terrific teacher. It was nice to know I was doing well. "I guess it's because I took a lot of typing."

"Maybe that plus some natural talent."

"Thanks, Miss McIntyre. Can I call up my letter now?"

She smiled at me. "The rest of the hour is yours, Katie."

I rushed back to my desk and started to punch in my computer code. But once again, I had to wait, this time because my best friend decided to stick her nose into my business.

"You're sure eager to get to that letter," Theresa said.

"Better hurry, Theresa. You've got four more problems," I told her.

Theresa ran her hand through her hair and sighed. "I'll never get this. It's like algebra and trig. Does this stuff really have anything to do with the real world?"

I laughed. "Yeah, I think so." She kept looking over my shoulder so I couldn't call up the letter.

"Katie, have you got something going on with your computer pal?" she asked me suddenly.

"Don't be silly, Theresa. I don't even know who it is." She looked at me and sort of smirked. Finally I asked, "Theresa, have you been blabbing around to anybody that you know my number or my pal's?"

She looked at me innocently. "No, I don't even remember those numbers. Why would you even ask me a thing like that?"

"I don't know. It's just that, well, I've got this feeling that my pal knows who I am."

"So what?" she said.

"What do you mean, so what?"

"I mean, big deal. I already know who mine is."

"You do?" I couldn't believe it.

"Yeah, I think so." Theresa looked at her keyboard pensively. "I think it's Amy Forslund from some clues I've been able to piece together. Who do you think yours is?"

"I'm not sure, but I think it's Pat."

"Pat Powers?" She smiled.

"Yeah."

"So, what's to be upset about?"

"Well, our letters have been kind of—personal."

Theresa looked shocked. "Personal? Like love letters?"

"No. Just—I don't know. We really talk about things."

"What kind of things? Tell me."

Boy, I had really painted myself into a corner this time. "I can't tell you, Theresa. I promised."

"Promised who?" she asked.

"STX."

"Who?" Theresa's face scrunched up.

"STX is my pal," I explained.

"Let me get this straight. You're writing love letters to Pat Powers, and you've promised to keep it a secret."

"No, no, no. They aren't love letters, and I'm not even sure that it is Pat."

"So why do you think it might be?" she asked me.

"All right. I know you're friendly with Pat, and one day he was at your locker talking to you and he looked at me kind of funny. I just thought that maybe by accident—you might have let slip what my number was."

Theresa looked hurt. "Katie, am I or am I not your best friend?"

"Of course you are," I said.

"Then how could you even think that I would do a thing like that?" She was really upset, and I felt terrible.

"I just thought that maybe, purely by accident,

you might have. I'm sorry, Theresa. It was awful of me."

Theresa smiled. "It's OK. Truth is, I might've blurted it out if I'd known it, but you only mentioned it once, and you know I'm terrible at remembering numbers." She leaned over and gave me a little hug. At that moment I felt that Theresa was the most sincere, sweet, and wonderful person on the whole earth. "So, why don't you show me one of those letters and maybe I can tell you if Pat wrote it or not," she said slyly.

What a nosy person that girl can be. "Theresa, I told you, I can't show you. I promised."

"Oh, come on, Katie. I'm your best friend," she pleaded.

"I can't," I replied.

"But if I could read one, I might be able to tell you if it was the kind of letter Pat would write."

"No, Theresa. Anyhow, I'm not sure I even want to know who it is. I promised not to try to find out."

"Boy, for strangers, you two sure are exchanging an awful lot of promises." She gave me a wink.

"It's nothing like that. It's just—look, Theresa, I just can't explain it right now," I said.

Theresa got real cold and turned back to her computer. "OK."

"Come on, Theresa. You're still my best friend." I wasn't getting through. "Haven't you got some secrets from me?"

"No."

"Well, all right! So I owe you one!"

She started working on her problems, and I called up my letter.

STX1150 to GHS5915

Dear GHS,

Hey, I really wish you wouldn't run yourself down like that. I'm not saying you can't tell me these things if you feel you have to. But right now, I can't think of another person whom I respect as much as I respect you. Your letters have shown me a warm, kind, sensitive person. Anyone would think of you as a treasure.

And as far as beauty goes—so what? Now, don't think that I'm being an idealist. I know how much easier things are for people who are born attractive, but that kind of beauty is only on the surface. It's what's on the inside that counts. My mother once told me that a person is like a glass. You can be a beautiful cut-crystal goblet or a plastic cup with Fred Flintstone on the outside, but when you get right down to it, it's what's in the cup that counts. I can tell that inside you're vintage champagne.

As for your other person, well, if he's just concerned with what you look like, then I wouldn't waste my time on him. Knowing you the way I do, I can't imagine you'd ever fall for somebody like that, anyway.

You know, the other day I realized I hadn't even wondered what you look like. I have absolutely no mental image of you. I guess the reason for that is, I've never needed one. The person I see coming across my computer TV screen once a week is beautiful enough to outshine any actress.

I guess all you really need right now is someone to convince you that you truly are beautiful, and since I'm your friend, it's probably my job. So, here goes. Dear GHS5915, I think you are really beautiful in every important way.

STX

Wow! I really hadn't been fishing for compliments when I'd written my last letter, but I'd sure gotten a computer screen full of them. I was just rereading that beautiful letter when I heard Theresa's voice behind me. "Incredible! I see what you mean about the letters being personal," she said.

I spun around. She had been reading over my shoulder. "Theresa! I told you this is private!"

"That really is an incredible letter."

"I can't believe that you'd do something like that. It's so sleazy, like reading someone else's mail or a diary or something."

"I'm sorry. I didn't mean—"

But I didn't let her finish. I turned off the computer and refused to speak to her the rest of the period. When she sat down, I quickly typed up an answer to STX's letter. I kept glancing at her, to see if she was watching but she was busy typing up her own letter. When the bell rang, I picked up my books and stormed out into the hall. Theresa stayed right on my heels. "Come on, Katie, don't be mad. I couldn't help myself." I kept walking. Finally she grabbed me by the shoulders and pushed me against a locker. "Look! I'm not going to let you do this. I am your best friend, and I know I did an awful thing, but if you're going to be mad at me, I want you to be mad at me to my face."

I looked at her. She was so serious, I couldn't help myself—I started to giggle. Then she joined me, and before too long both of us were really laughing hard. After we calmed down, I told her all about STX. I *had* to, promises or no promises. She practically knew already, anyway.

"You've got to swear to me, Theresa, that you will never, ever tell anybody else about this."

"I swear."

"Really, because it's very serious to me."

"I do, I promise. I think it's really neat, Katie."

"It's turned out pretty well so far. This has meant so much to me, whoever STX is and whatever happens after this assignment, even if I never find out who STX is . . ."

Suddenly I felt very sad. I guess I'd always known that someday this thing with STX would be over, but I'd never really thought about it. I felt as if I were losing someone important to me. Someone really important.

Chapter Eight

"Theresa, do the small forks go on the outside or on the inside?" I called to her in the kitchen.

"Silverware goes in the order that you use it, Katie. The small forks are for salad, which we'll eat first, so they go on the outside," she yelled back.

I laid out the rest of the silverware and set some candles on the table. When everything was set, it looked beautiful. The whole house was perfect, with flowers everywhere. Theresa and her family live in a beautiful home on the lake. It's a big old house with tons of windows and two fireplaces. The beamed ceilings are high, and the walls are hung with beautiful artworks. All the furniture is modern but very comfortable.

We'd done a really nice job on the decorations. There were no big paper Christmas trees or Santas. Instead, we'd set candles and fresh flowers on every available surface. We had a big punch bowl set up in the living room with fresh fruit floating in it and real glasses, not plastic cups. We'd pushed all the furniture back against the walls in the den so everyone could dance after dinner. The dining room was the best, though. We'd set the long oak table with a white linen tablecloth and matching napkins. The candles made the glasses shine and sparkle. Theresa's mom had even bought some nonalcoholic champagne made from apple cider to have with dinner.

Theresa looked very pretty in her satin dress and her hair piled up on her head. I have to admit, I looked pretty special myself. I had on a wonderful green silk dress. The skirt was very full and came to just below my knees and the front was cut a little low.

Of course, as we finished making the dinner, both of us were wearing aprons. "Give me a hand here, Katie," Theresa said, pulling the salad out of the refrigerator and looking for a place to set it down. I cleared a space on the counter.

We probably had enough food for a small army, but it all looked scrumptious. The first course was going to be fresh melon with little slices of strawberry. Next, we had planned a crisp spinach salad. Then we'd serve the turkey, which was stuffed with wild rice, broccoli with cream sauce, and twice-baked potatoes stuffed with cheese. For dessert, as if we'd be able to eat anything after that feast, we'd bought a black forest cake.

Theresa surveyed the counter and wrinkled her forehead. "Do you think there's enough food?"

"For what country?" I asked. "Relax, Theresa. Everything looks beautiful. So do you."

"Thanks. You look pretty wonderful yourself. That dress is going to knock Bobby over." She gave me a big smile.

"I hope so."

Theresa whipped off her apron. "Come on. I want to sit down for a couple of minutes before everyone gets here. All I have to do is take the turkey out of the oven and carve it."

"Theresa, you really are amazing."

"Why?"

"I can't believe you know how to do all this stuff."

"Well, I love cooking. I guess I got that from my

mom. She's a real maniac about entertaining. She thinks it's a lost art, so all of us kids were trained on how to do it right."

We went into the living room and sat there quietly for a minute with just the logs on the fire crackling. It was all going to be so perfect. Bobby had accepted right away when Theresa called him. He hadn't said a thing about Tammy. Besides Bobby, we had invited Alan Powell, a guy Theresa sometimes goes out with, our friends Chris and Edwina and their boyfriends, and Pat, and some other kids from school. We purposely didn't invite everyone in pairs so it wouldn't look like we were trying to put Bobby and me together.

We'd invited everyone for eight o'clock, so I was a little surprised when the doorbell rang at quarter to. Theresa was in the kitchen, I answered it.

Bobby stood in the doorway, looking a little sheepish. "Hi," he said. "I'm sorry I'm a little early, but I didn't want to be late, so I left my house a little too early. And the truth is, I've been sitting in my car in the driveway for about fifteen minutes. Aren't you going to ask me in?"

I started to laugh. He looked so funny standing there, holding a bunch of flowers and babbling about sitting in his car in the driveway. "Yes, of course. Come in," I said, laughing.

He walked into the foyer and took off his coat, which I put in the closet. He was wearing a beautiful gray three-piece suit. He tugged at his tie a little. Like I said, Bobby is not a natural for a suit and tie, but he did look terrific. He had a flower in his buttonhole that had gotten crushed a bit by his coat.

"You're a little mashed," I said.

"What?"

"Your flower. Your coat smashed it down a little."

He looked down at it and laughed. "Yeah, I guess so. This party sounded so elegant that I thought a flower would be a good idea."

"Here, let me fix it." I walked over to him and started to rearrange the flower. Suddenly I became aware of how close I was to him. I think he did, too, because both of us were quiet for a second. "There, it's as good as new," I said finally.

He smiled. "Thanks, Katie. Where's Theresa?"

"In the kitchen. Come on."

I led him through the house and into the kitchen, where Theresa was attacking the turkey. It looked as if the bird was fighting back. She looked up at us and smiled. "Hi, Bobby. You're a little early."

Bobby and I exchanged a look. "It's a long

story," he said. "What are you doing to that poor turkey?"

"I'm trying to carve it."

He walked over and gently took the knife and fork out of her hands. "Here, I'm an expert at this. My father says I'm so good, I ought to be a surgeon. But I don't agree. All my patients so far have ended up being eaten."

Theresa noticed the flowers Bobby had handed me. "Oh, you brought flowers. How sweet." She took them from me and put them in a vase of water.

Bobby really did carve the turkey like an expert and before too long, there was a platter of meat, perfectly arranged, sitting on a hot tray.

Theresa looked at the platter and smiled. "Bobby Allen, is there anything you can't do?"

Bobby looked a little embarrassed. "Sure, lots of things," he mumbled.

After that our other guests started arriving. At first all of us were a litle stiff because all the guys were wearing ties and suits and all the girls were in their best dresses. You know how it is at a prom early in the evening. Everyone walks around trying not to get dirty. Things always loosen up after a while.

That's what happened at our party. Alan started telling jokes, Chris played a couple of songs on the piano, and Pat did a really funny impersonation of one of the biology teachers. At about eight-thirty we all went in to the dining room for the meal.

Everyone oohed and aahed over the table and the food and the fake champagne. It was all too wonderful. Theresa sat at the head of the table, and Alan sat at the other end. Bobby and I sat opposite each other. Alan stood up and made a very sweet toast to Theresa and me. He called us "our two beautiful hostesses." Bobby and I talked together all through dinner. It was so easy and natural, I didn't even think about which fork I was using.

I was rather surprised when Bobby opened his mouth and asked, "What did you use to season this stuffing? Tarragon and parsley?"

"How did you know?" I asked in amazement.

"Oh," he said quietly, "I like to cook. I guess it's because I like to eat." He smiled and put a piece of broccoli into his mouth.

Ted was sitting next to Bobby. "Not me," he said. "I love to eat, but about all I can make is a peanut butter and jelly sandwich."

Bobby looked at me. "What about you, Katie? You like to cook?"

"I like to eat more, I'm afraid."

"Katie did a lot of the dinner," Theresa said.

"Oh, I helped a little, that's all."

"Well, it's terrific." Bobby looked straight into my eyes.

I didn't look away. "Thanks."

Every once in a while I had to fight off the urge to excuse myself from the table and go into another room and scream. It was all so romantic.

After dinner nobody had room for dessert, but the sight of that big, luscious cake changed their minds. After the cake we all just sat around. We were too full to move. Finally Alan got up. "Well, it's about time we worked all that food off," he said. He went into the den and put on the rock 'n' roll tape that Theresa had made especially for the party. He turned it up really loud. That got us moving. First we all helped with the dishes in time to the music. With so many people helping, it took no time at all until the dining room and kitchen were spotless and the dishwasher was full and chugging away.

Then the party moved into the den for dancing. Bobby and I danced together for what seemed like hours. He's really a terrific dancer. He caught on quickly to a few new steps I showed him. Pretty soon everyone cleared off the floor just to watch us. Our minds and bodies were working together perfectly. He knew just where I was going a second before I did. When the song ended, everyone applauded. The dance floor filled up again, but Bobby and I sat down to catch our breaths.

Theresa and Alan whirled over to us. "Hey, what's the matter?" Theresa asked. "Can't you keep up with us, wild dancers that you are?"

"Just winding up for a big finish," Bobby said. He stood up and offered me his hand. "Care to show them what dancing's really about?"

"Give me another second. I'm still out of breath."

He laughed and turned to Theresa. "It's nice of your parents to let us use your house like this."

Theresa's parents are really great. Her dad is a lawyer, and her mom teaches art at a nearby college. I love how they trust Theresa to make her own decisions. For instance, I don't know if my folks would turn over our house to a bunch of my friends and then disappear for the evening, but that's exactly what Theresa's parents did. They were upstairs in their bedroom, but they hadn't come down once.

"I think so too," said Theresa. "Have you gone out to look at the lake?"

Bobby sat back down. "No, not yet."

"Oh, why don't you. Katie knows the way."

Wasn't that about as subtle as a bag of bricks over the head?

Bobby turned to me. "Do you mind? I'd love to see it in winter. I've only seen it in summer when I used to mow the lawn."

I glared at Theresa, who just smiled back. "I could use some fresh air," I said, turning back to Bobby and smiling.

It was very cold, so we bundled up in our jackets. We walked through the back of the house to the terrace and out onto the lawn. The house sits on top of a hill, so you don't see the lake until you get to the edge of the lawn. Then you have to go down a flight of stairs to the beach.

The lake is always beautiful, but I think it's the prettiest in the cold months before it freezes over. True, you can't do anything like swim or water ski, but it's just so peaceful, so still. The sky was velvet black and peppered with stars. The air was crystal sharp and clear.

We stood at the edge of the lawn at the top of the stairs, looking out on the wide, black expanse of water. I glanced at Bobby. He was staring straight ahead, a little hint of a smile on his lips. When he spoke, it was almost a whisper. "I would like my whole life to look like this." Then he looked at me, a little embarrassed, as if he had forgotten I was there. "It's just a game I play," he explained shyly.

"Tell me about it," I said softly.

He was quiet for a moment, and then he laughed. "Sometimes I wonder: if my life could be just one picture, what would I want it to look like?"

We locked eyes for a second, then we both looked straight ahead again. "And this is what you want your life to look like?"

He was quiet for a second. "It changes. Sometimes it's like this. Sometimes it's more active, like halftime at a football game. Sometimes it's— different things." He was quiet again. He glanced down the stairs. "Want to go down to the beach?"

"There isn't much of a beach there now. In the winter the lake is high. But we can go, anyway."

We started down the shaky wooden stairs. Every once in a while, Bobby would offer me his hand to steady me. I was still wearing my high heels, so I needed his help. Finally we were on the sand. Bobby went to the edge of the water and skipped a few stones. It was very dark, so we had to listen closely to count the skips.

"How many that time?" he asked me.

"I counted four."

He laughed. "You're out of your mind. That was six at least."

"You wish."

Bobby walked over to where I was standing, and we wandered down the beach in silence. "You cold?" he asked me.

"A little," I said.

He took his muffler off and wrapped it around my neck. "There, better?"

"Yes, much."

"So, tell me. We've become friends in the last few weeks, haven't we?"

"Sure," I said. If he only knew.

"So, tell me about yourself. It seems to me that you know an awful lot about Bobby Allen, with football and all, but I know very little about Katie McNamara."

"Well, you know about my family—"

"No, I don't, just your dad."

"My mom is an architect. She's really a terrific person. And then I've got a little brother, Charlie. He's all right when he isn't getting into my stuff or listening in to my phone calls or being a general pain, which is practically always."

He laughed. "And what about you, Katie?"

"Hmm, that's a hard one," I said with a laugh. "How should I describe myself? Well, I'm a pretty good student. I play a mean game of racquet-ball."

"Really? We should play sometime."

"Great, that sounds like fun."

He smiled. "So? What else?"

"I don't know what to say," I said shyly.

All of a sudden I thought about STX. This was exactly the kind of thing we'd been talking about. Here I had the perfect opportunity to talk to Bobby, and all that I could do was stammer about my grades and racquetball.

It was funny, but the thought of STX made me feel something else, too. I felt a little guilty, as if I were cheating on STX just by being out there with Bobby. No matter how much I cared about Bobby, I had developed a real relationship with STX. If I got close to Bobby, would I somehow be hurting STX?

It was crazy. I mean, I wasn't even sure who STX was. And besides, he was interested in someone else. But most important, by opening myself up to Bobby, wouldn't I be excluding STX? The term was going to end in a few weeks, anyway, and I'd probably never even know who STX was.

STX probably would have been proud of me if I'd talked to Bobby the way I talked to him. That's what STX had been saying I should do. So if I took his advice, what right did he have to be upset about it? When I realized what I was thinking, I stopped myself. How could I be mad at STX? The poor guy hadn't even done anything.

I was really thinking nonsense. I decided right then and there, that I was going to open myself up to Bobby. He wanted to know what Katie McNamara was all about, and I was going to tell him. It was just at that moment that Theresa called down to us from the lawn above. "Katie? Bobby? Are you guys down there?"

"Yeah?" I called up. What a time for my best friend to show up.

"Bobby has a phone call."

Bobby turned to me. "A phone call? I wonder who it could be?"

He offered me his hand, and we walked down the beach and up the stairs. Theresa was waiting at the top. "Must be cold down there," she said.

"Not too bad," Bobby answered.

Theresa gave me a sly little smile, but I just shook my head. We walked across the lawn and back into the house. "You can grab the phone over there if you want," Theresa said, pointing to the kitchen wall phone.

"Thanks," Bobby said. Theresa and I went into the living room.

"Anything interesting happen out there?" Theresa asked me.

"Nothing much. We had a nice talk."

"Listen, Katie—" Theresa said, a funny catch in her voice.

Just then Bobby walked over to us. He looked a little pale, embarrassed. "Katie, Theresa, I'm sorry. I've got to take off."

"So soon?" I asked, disappointment showing on my face.

"Yeah. I'm sorry. Something just came up."

Theresa was strangely quiet.

"Well, sure," I said. "I hope nothing's wrong."

Bobby smiled weakly. "No, it's nothing. I just have to get going. I really had a terrific time."

I could feel my heart turning into Jell-O as he said those last, wonderful words. "It was a nice walk on the beach," I said softly. We walked to the door.

"I hope we can continue that talk sometime," he said.

"Yeah. Me, too."

He leaned over and kissed me on the cheek. "Thanks again. Merry Christmas."

"Thanks. You, too."

I watched him walk down the driveway. In a

second he was gone. Then I went and found Theresa, who was in the kitchen unloading the dishwasher. Everyone else was still noisily dancing in the den. "Well, the party's still in full gear," I said.

Theresa didn't stop what she was doing. "Yeah," she said hollowly.

"I hope nothing's wrong with Bobby. He was quiet when he left."

"Yeah," she said again.

I grabbed her hands and turned her to face me. "Theresa, what is wrong? You sound as if you've lost your best friend."

She was quiet for a second, then she looked up. "Katie, it was Tammy Sawyer on the phone," she blurted out.

There was a moment of complete silence. "Oh," I said. My throat closed up over any other words I might have said.

The strangled silence was broken when Alan burst into the room. "Hey, you two, there's lots of music going on in there and not enough people to dance to it."

Theresa looked at me, and I returned her look with a smile. "Let's go in. I feel like dancing," she said.

Theresa may have felt like dancing, but I felt like crying.

Chapter Nine

Ok, so it was Tammy Sawyer on the phone.

But maybe she didn't have anything to do with Bobby leaving early. Maybe he just had to get home. Maybe his folks needed the car. Maybe he had studying to do. Maybe he was leaving anyway and the phone call from Tammy was just a coincidence. Maybe Mark Twain would drop over to the house to help me with my English lit assignment.

What was going on? If Bobby and Tammy were still going together, Bobby sure wasn't acting like it. I mean, I may not be the most experienced person when it comes to romance, but I knew what was happening out there on the beach.

Something was going on between Bobby and me. If he and Tammy were back together, wouldn't he have made that clear somehow? What's more, I hadn't heard anything at school about a big reconciliation.

One answer—and one that I hated to think about—was that Bobby was just letting both Tammy and me think he was interested in us. But I couldn't really believe that. Not Bobby. He definitely wasn't the type to be so dishonest. But what other answer could there be?

Maybe he felt we were just friends, like Theresa and Pat Powers. Maybe he couldn't see how I felt about him because he thought of us as buddies.

I discussed all the possibilities with Theresa, of course, after everyone left that night. She thought I should just come out and tell him how I felt. But I didn't know if I could do that. I mean, which would be worse, having the possibility that he did like me or knowing for sure that he didn't? Of course, there was the chance that he would take me in his arms, kiss me, and tell me that I was the girl he'd been waiting for all his life.

After the party Theresa and I took off our beautiful dresses, got into nightgowns, and snuggled into bed. It was quite late, but I had planned to spend the night at her house, anyway.

"About Bobby," she said. "I would hate to think he was playing games with you, Katie, but that's what it looks like."

"I can't believe it," I answered her.

"Well, then what do you think is going on?"

"I don't know, Theresa. If I did, I wouldn't be awake at two in the morning talking to you."

Theresa was quiet for a second. "Then you don't think he wants to go out with you and Tammy at the same time?"

I got up out of bed and started to pace. "I don't know, I just don't know." Then I added, "But I do think he really likes me."

"Oh, yeah?"

"Yeah. You should have heard him out on the beach. He's so sensitive. He was really interested in getting to know me." I shook my head and sat down on my bed. "I don't know what's going on."

"Maybe you should ask your friend," she said.

"Who?" I asked.

"You know, the computer."

"Oh, STX. That's not a bad idea."

We were both quiet for a second. I didn't notice that Theresa was drifting off to sleep, and her mention of STX brought a whole other problem into my mind.

"Theresa?" I asked.

"What? Huh?"

"Were you asleep?"

"No, it's OK. What?"

"Listen. Do you think it's possible to have a crush on someone you really don't even know?"

"You mean, like when I decided I was in love with David Bowie?" she asked.

"No, even more weird. Someone you've never even seen."

"How could you be in love with somebody you've never even seen?" Theresa laughed and rolled onto her stomach.

"Well, let's say you knew how his mind worked, but you didn't know anything else." It sounded dumb even to me. I sighed and got back in bed.

"Well, that's really important. But then again, you'd hate to get hooked up with somebody who never washed his hair or brushed his teeth or stuff like that."

"You're right," I said. But then I added, "That shouldn't be important if the guy was a good person."

"No, it shouldn't be, but it is," Theresa said flatly. She rolled over to face the wall. Then she snapped back and sat up. "Wait a second. You're not falling in love with this STX thing, are you?"

"Theresa?" I asked.

"What? Huh?"

"Were you asleep?"

"No, it's OK. What?"

"Listen. Do you think it's possible to have a crush on someone you really don't even know?"

"You mean, like when I decided I was in love with David Bowie?" she asked.

"No, even more weird. Someone you've never even seen."

"How could you be in love with somebody you've never even seen?" Theresa laughed and rolled onto her stomach.

"Well, let's say you knew how his mind worked, but you didn't know anything else." It sounded dumb even to me. I sighed and got back in bed.

"Well, that's really important. But then again, you'd hate to get hooked up with somebody who never washed his hair or brushed his teeth or stuff like that."

"You're right," I said. But then I added, "That shouldn't be important if the guy was a good person."

"No, it shouldn't be, but it is," Theresa said flatly. She rolled over to face the wall. Then she snapped back and sat up. "Wait a second. You're not falling in love with this STX thing, are you?"

Chapter Nine

O<small>K,</small> so it was Tammy Sawyer on the phone.

But maybe she didn't have anything to do with Bobby leaving early. Maybe he just had to get home. Maybe his folks needed the car. Maybe he had studying to do. Maybe he was leaving anyway and the phone call from Tammy was just a coincidence. Maybe Mark Twain would drop over to the house to help me with my English lit assignment.

What was going on? If Bobby and Tammy were still going together, Bobby sure wasn't acting like it. I mean, I may not be the most experienced person when it comes to romance, but I knew what was happening out there on the beach.

Something was going on between Bobby and me. If he and Tammy were back together, wouldn't he have made that clear somehow? What's more, I hadn't heard anything at school about a big reconciliation.

One answer—and one that I hated to think about—was that Bobby was just letting both Tammy and me think he was interested in us. But I couldn't really believe that. Not Bobby. He definitely wasn't the type to be so dishonest. But what other answer could there be?

Maybe he felt we were just friends, like Theresa and Pat Powers. Maybe he couldn't see how I felt about him because he thought of us as buddies.

I discussed all the possibilities with Theresa, of course, after everyone left that night. She thought I should just come out and tell him how I felt. But I didn't know if I could do that. I mean, which would be worse, having the possibility that he did like me or knowing for sure that he didn't? Of course, there was the chance that he would take me in his arms, kiss me, and tell me that I was the girl he'd been waiting for all his life.

After the party Theresa and I took off our beautiful dresses, got into nightgowns, and snuggled into bed. It was quite late, but I had planned to spend the night at her house, anyway.

"About Bobby," she said. "I would hate to think he was playing games with you, Katie, but that's what it looks like."

"I can't believe it," I answered her.

"Well, then what do you think is going on?"

"I don't know, Theresa. If I did, I wouldn't be awake at two in the morning talking to you."

Theresa was quiet for a second. "Then you don't think he wants to go out with you and Tammy at the same time?"

I got up out of bed and started to pace. "I don't know, I just don't know." Then I added, "But I do think he really likes me."

"Oh, yeah?"

"Yeah. You should have heard him out on the beach. He's so sensitive. He was really interested in getting to know me." I shook my head and sat down on my bed. "I don't know what's going on."

"Maybe you should ask your friend," she said.

"Who?" I asked.

"You know, the computer."

"Oh, STX. That's not a bad idea."

We were both quiet for a second. I didn't notice that Theresa was drifting off to sleep, and her mention of STX brought a whole other problem into my mind.

"He's not a thing. He's a person," I answered.

Theresa threw her pillow at me. "You are absolutely crackers, you know that?"

I threw the pillow back, "Look, Theresa, I'm not saying I'm in love with STX. I'm just saying—oh, I don't know. I'm a mess!"

"You sure are." She sighed. "What brought all this on?"

"Oh, I don't know. It's just that—well, tonight when Bobby and I were out there on the beach, I started to open up to him. And all of a sudden, I felt kind of bad about STX, like I was replacing him or something."

"Katie McNamara, this is absolutely, positively absurd. Look, STX is a friend, right?"

"Yeah."

"And I'm your friend, too, right?"

"Right," I answered.

"Well, did you feel like you were replacing me out there?"

"No, but with you it's different," I said.

"Thanks a lot." Theresa turned away.

"That's not what I mean, Theresa, and you know it."

She laughed. "I just don't understand why you're making all this fuss about somebody you'll probably never meet." I started to interrupt her, but she stopped me. "Katie, you know that, not counting Christmas break, there are only two more weeks of the term. Are you going to tell this STX who you are?"

"I don't know. I haven't decided."

"What does he think?" she asked.

"We haven't really talked about it."

"Well, suppose you do. What do you think is going to happen? I mean, this is a pretty romantic situation, two mysterious friends and all. How will your friendship change if you just start a normal relationship?"

"I don't know."

"I'll tell you. If you're both mature enough, it won't change. If it wasn't meant to be, it will just fade away. No big deal."

"I guess you're right."

"Of course, I'm right. That's why I'm your best friend. It's my job to be right." She sounded very smug.

I laughed. "Of course you are. You always are. What would I do without you?"

"We'd both probably get some sleep," she moaned.

"That's true." I laughed, then closed my eyes. I was quiet for a moment. Then I said, "Theresa?"

"Yeah?"

"I don't want you to feel like I've replaced you

with STX. I tell you lots of things I don't tell him."

"I know. I've got some secrets from you, too, I guess."

I sat up. "You do? Like what?"

A pillow hit me square in the face. "Shut up and go to sleep," Theresa said.

I giggled. "Shup," I said.

Chapter Ten

The Sunday before we had to return to school from Christmas break, I was a vegetable most of the day. It's really hard to gear up to go back to school. I tried to trade off with my dad to make dinner, but he wouldn't hear of it. With my eyes half closed, I managed to slap something together, a tuna salad.

"Dinner is less than inspired, Katie," Dad said at the table that evening as he took another forkful of my strange meal.

"I told you you should have traded with me," I said.

Charlie helped himself to seconds. "I like it for once," he said.

"Great," I answered.

"Charlie, don't talk with your mouth full." That was Mom.

Charlie smiled. "It's tuna, right? That's seafood." He opened his full mouth. "See, food."

"Mom? Can't we send him to college early or something?" I moaned.

Mom glared at Charlie. "I'm willing to excuse that last spectacle on account of your age. Once more, and you're grounded until your eighteenth birthday."

"Nobody in this family has a sense of humor," Charlie said to his plate.

After a couple minutes of silence, the phone rang. I excused myself from the table and got it. It was Theresa.

"Katie?" Theresa practically screamed into the phone.

"Yeah, hi, Theresa," I said. "What's up?"

"I just talked to Ted Dunn, and you'll never guess what he just told me." Her voice sounded really excited.

"What?" I asked.

"The Varsity Club just took a vote of all its members on the phone and decided to make their prom a turnabout."

"What?" I was starting to wake up.

"Yeah, a turnabout. The girls are supposed to ask the guys."

"You're kidding."

"Would I kid about something like that?"

"Katie, dinner isn't finished," Mom called from the kitchen.

"OK, I'm coming," I called, then I turned back to the phone. "Theresa, I'll call you back in a while. I'm in the middle of dinner."

"OK, sorry. Bye."

After I hung up, I felt as if I could fly back to the table. This was just what I'd been waiting for. I had decided that Theresa was right: if I wanted Bobby, I was just going to have to go after him. This was perfect. Monday morning, first thing, I was going to ask Bobby to go with me to the prom. If he said yes, fantastic. If he said no, well, I'd deal with that when and if it happened.

When I got back to the table, Mom had already cleared it. She was bringing out some strawberry ice cream for dessert.

"Who was that?" she asked.

"Theresa."

Mom started scooping the ice cream into bowls and handing them around to us. "She must have said something wonderful. You look like you're going to burst any second." I giggled into my ice cream. "Well, are you going to tell me about it?" she prodded.

"It's nothing. Theresa just found out that the Varsity Prom is going to be a turnabout," I replied.

"Oh." Mom scooped a bowlful for Charle. Then it sunk in. "Oh!"

Dad looked up at us. "What's that all about?"

"The Varsity Prom is going to be a turnabout," my mom told him. She and I exchanged a smile. Mom knew all about Bobby, so she realized what this meant to me.

"So?" Dad asked.

"That's all," I said. Mom and I burst out laughing.

Charlie turned to Dad. "What's going on?"

Dad went back to his ice cream. "I haven't the faintest idea."

"What's a turnabout?" Charlie asked.

Dad kept on eating. "It's a dance where the girls get to ask the boys."

"Why's Katie so excited?"

"I don't know. I suppose she's got some poor guy on the line, and this'll help her reel him in," my dad said.

"What if she asks him and he says no?" Charlie asked.

"He won't say no," Dad replied.

Charlie wasn't going to be stopped. "Why, Dad?"

"Because people just don't," Dad answered.

"Why?" Charlie asked.

I guess Dad couldn't think of a good answer. "I don't know."

"I thought you were supposed to know everything," Charlie said.

Dad finished his ice cream. "Who told you that?"

"You did." Charlie had him trapped.

"Well, I changed my mind," Dad said.

Charlie was quiet for a second. Then he muttered into his ice-cream bowl. "Just when you think you know how to play the game, they come along and change the rules."

Monday morning was a nightmare. The problem was what to wear. Suddenly everything in my closet looked terrible. None of the colors went together. Everything was either too big or too small. My hair looked awful. I had to do my makeup twice. I was too busy even to think about the shoe problem. I ended up sitting on the edge of my bed in my slip, staring into my closet, hoping something would just fall out.

My mom came into the room. "Hey, what's

going on? Theresa's going to be here in a minute."

"I haven't got anything to wear," I said hopelessly.

Mom looked into my packed closet and raised an eyebrow. "What do you call all of this?"

"Junk," I replied.

"What about your new skirt?" She held the skirt up.

"It's too tight," I moaned.

"That yellow dress? You look very pretty in that," she said.

"Yellow? With my skin color, I'd look like a fish."

"Oh, come on, Katie. All these clothes were fine two weeks ago."

I dropped back onto my bed and put a pillow over my head. "Something happened during the night."

"What?" she asked.

"I got ugly," I replied.

She sighed. "You are not ugly." She dove back into the closet. "Here, I love this white shirt."

I looked up. She was holding an oversized, long-sleeved white blouse I'd gotten for Christmas. I don't know why I hadn't thought of wearing it, "Yeah, that's OK, but what do I wear it with?"

"Wear your jeans, the cropped ones, and accent it all with red. How about that wide belt and your short red boots."

The outfit began to pull together in my mind. "Yeah. I guess that would look pretty good."

She walked out of the room. "Give it a shot," she said over her shoulder, "and hurry. You don't want to be late."

I got up and put the outfit on. Good old Mom. It was perfect. I finished checking myself out in the mirror for the eighteenth time just as Theresa pulled up outside the house and honked. I grabbed my coat and ran out through the kitchen. Mom and Dad were having coffee.

"Do you want something to take with you in the car?" Mom asked.

"No, I'd probably just spill it on myself."

I gave them both kisses and ran out the door.

Theresa's car was waiting at the curb. Even from outside, I could hear every word of David Bowie's newest album. She wasn't in love with him anymore, but she was still a real Bowie freak. I threw open the door and jumped in. "Hi."

"Hi," She stepped on the gas and pulled away from the curb. "Boy, Katie, you look terrific."

"Thanks."

"Listen, I think you'd better ask Bobby first

thing. Don't wait until later in the day because you might not get a chance."

"Theresa, you're making this into a big deal, and it isn't. I am going to ask Bobby to the dance today, but I'm not going to break my neck doing it. If he goes with me, fine, and if someone else asks him first, well, that's the way it goes."

Theresa gave me a look. "You're sure being awful cool about this all of a sudden."

"That's just the way it is, Theresa. You can't go around killing yourself all the time over a guy."

"I guess you're right." Theresa pulled the car into a Standard station.

"What are you doing?"

"I've got to get some gas."

"Are you out of your mind! We might be late, and Tammy Sawyer could get to him first!"

Theresa laughed. "There's my Katie. I was beginning to worry."

"Come on, Theresa. Hurry."

"OK." Still laughing, she got out of the car and started to fill the tank.

I was lost in my thoughts and the music, and I guess I really jumped when I heard a knock on the car window. I looked over and saw Bobby laughing on the other side. I lowered the music and rolled the window down. "Hi, lady. Check your oil?" he asked.

"Hi. What are you doing here?"

"Same as you guys. Filling up. Hi, Theresa."

Theresa yelled from the other side of the car. "Hi, Bobby."

"Hey, thanks again for that great dinner party. Sorry I had to take off so quickly."

"Oh, that's OK," Theresa said. She finished putting the gas in the car. Then she gave me her sly smile and said, "Katie, would you get the windshield while I pay for this?"

"I'll do it," Bobby said.

I started to get out of the car. "No, it's OK." I was moving pretty quickly, and I didn't see that Theresa had pulled up too close to the pumps. When I threw open the door, I hit a display of oil cans and sent them rolling. "Wonderful!" I said.

Bobby and I started running all over, catching the cans before they got a chance to roll into the street.

I carried the last of the cans to where Bobby was setting up the display again. "Wow, am I a klutz," I said.

"Oh, don't worry about it. It could have happened to anybody." Bobby stood up. He had a grease spot on one knee where he'd been kneeling down.

"Oh, Bobby, your pants. I'm so sorry."

He looked down at the spot. "It's nothing. It'll

come out." He picked up a bucket of water and handed me the window washer. "Here. You wash, I'll dry."

"Sure." I was trying to maintain some kind of dignity. But that dissolved completely when I took the window washer away from him. I wasn't watching what I was doing, and as he handed me the bucket, I dropped it. Water splashed all over his pants and shoes.

I looked at Bobby, grease spotted and wet, and I did the only intelligent, rational thing anyone could do in a situation like that. I began to laugh uncontrollably. After a second, Bobby joined me.

I figured it could only go uphill from there, so when I finally caught my breath, I just turned to Bobby and blurted out, "Bobby, since the Varsity Prom is going to be a turnabout, would you like to go with me?"

He was quiet for a moment. Then he smiled at me. "I think I'd like that very much."

"You would?" I tried not to gasp, but I think I did.

"I would." He laughed. Both of us looked at each other for a second and laughed a little more. "Well, it's been fun." Bobby looked down at his wet pants. "I think I'd better take off. I should go home and change."

"Oh, Bobby, I'm so sorry," I said.

"Don't worry about it," he said. "It's no big deal. I'll see you later." He put gas into his car and walked off to pay.

I got into the car as Theresa opened her door. "What just happened?" she asked me.

"I'm not sure, but I think it was something wonderful."

Chapter Eleven

They tell you that when it rains, it pours. Well, that day the good news kept dropping on me. I was walking on air when I walked into my computer class. Then I called up STX's letter.

STX1150 to GHS5915

Dear GHS,

It's funny to think that you won't get this letter until after Christmas vacation. After that, we'll only have one more week of correspondence until finals week. How do you feel about that? I feel terrible. I've never had a relationship like this before. I don't know if I'll ever have one like it again. I still have no idea who you are except that you're a girl.

More and more I find myself thinking about you. Of course, I can always tell you who I am, and then it won't have to end, but that frightens me a little. I wish I could talk to somebody about it, but the only person I can really open up to is you.

I know that's stupid, but I can't help it. I just don't know if I want to find out who you are and run the risk that our future relationship won't live up to this one. It may be silly, but you have to remember, I've just come out of a relationship that started out wonderfully and ended up as a nightmare. I'm really afraid of having all that happen again. Especially with you.

Right now you are probably thinking that I am a real lunatic, and I can't say that I blame you for thinking that. You know, I almost wrote my name down just now, but I thought about it and decided that it might be a better idea if I heard what you had to say before I did. Since we have so little time, let's write every day this week instead of just once more. Let me know how you feel.

STX1150

Isn't that amazing? STX and I were having identical thoughts. Our relationship really was special. But that didn't help me decide what to do next. *Wow,* I thought, *this had to happen just now, when things between Bobby and me are looking so good.* All of a sudden I was all confused again.

Miss McIntyre started class, so I had to put off writing my reply to STX until class was almost over. I thought it would give me the time I needed to think up an answer. But when the bell rang, I still didn't have an idea of what to write. I sat in front of that TV screen hoping that somehow the words would magically materialize.

"Katie, aren't you going to be late for your next class?"

I turned around to find Miss McIntyre standing behind me. "Oh, it's OK, Miss McIntyre. All I have is a study hall."

"What's the problem?" she asked.

"It's nothing," I said. "I just have to answer my pal's letter, and I can't think of what to write."

"Well, it shouldn't be that difficult."

"No, it shouldn't." I tried my best to smile.

We were both quiet for a second. Then she asked me, "Katie, is something wrong?"

I looked at her. As I said, Miss McIntyre is a really wonderful teacher. She sounded so concerned about me that I suddenly felt I could tell her everything. So I poured it out, the whole story about STX and Bobby and the letters. "This is what I got today." I recalled the letter to the screen and let her read it.

After she finished, she smiled. "Well, I must say, I never expected this assignment to have these results."

"Neither did I."

She pulled up a chair next to mine and sat down. "I don't know if you're asking me for advice or not; and if you are, I really don't know what to say."

"Anything would help, believe me."

"Well." She took a long, deep breath. "It seems to me that your relationship with STX1150 has a wonderful base. You two have always been honest with each other, and that, Katie, is rare. Maybe that's your answer right there. Just tell him the truth, the way you've told me."

"I don't know. . . ."

"All you can tell him is how you feel."

I sighed. "I should have known you'd give me good advice."

She stood up and squeezed my shoulder reassuringly. "I've got to finish a lesson plan. I'm going down to the teachers' lounge to do it. You take all the time you need."

She started to walk out, but I stopped her. "Miss McIntyre?"

"Yes?"

"If I decide not to tell STX who I am, would you tell me who he is?"

"Katie, I would if I could, but I can't."

"I understand."

"No, you see, I can't tell you because I don't know myself."

"You're kidding."

"I told you the first day of class that the computer matched everyone up. I don't have the program anymore."

"Oh," I said. "How many students are in your sections?"

"A hundred and twelve." That shut me up for a second. Miss McIntyre broke the silence. "I'm sorry, Katie."

"Oh, that's OK," I said, sighing. "I shouldn't have been asking you anyhow. I promised STX I wouldn't."

She started out of the room again. "Well, good luck."

When she was gone, I sat alone in the room with nothing but the computer keyboard, my TV screen, and a head full of knotted ideas.

OK, I thought, *I have to analyze this situation. I am crazy about Bobby Allen, and I think he is starting to notice me. I have a date with him for the Varsity Prom and that's further than I ever thought I'd get with him. True, I had to ask him, but he did say yes! Of course, there's the problem with Tammy Sawyer.*

Now, here is STX1150. He's telling me that he thinks there might be more between us than a bunch of wire and silicon chips. The problem is, I don't know how to tell him that he might be right. In fact, I don't even want to right now, when everything seems to be going so well with Bobby.

Of course, there was the possibility that things would go terribly with Bobby. We'd never been out alone together. It might all turn out to be wrong. But then I could go back to STX. Only that would be after the term ended, so if I didn't tell him who I was now, he'd be gone, too. Then where would I be? On the other hand, maybe STX and I would get together and find out that it was better between us when we were faceless letters. Maybe a regular relationship wouldn't work out.

Finally I decided to do just what Miss McIntyre had suggested.

GHS5915 to STX1150

Dear STX,

Let me start by saying that your letter meant a lot to me. Yes, I've been feeling all of those things, too. I think about you, about us, quite a bit. More now than before. The problem is, things have just started working out well for me with my other person. I'm not saying it's perfect, but at least it's developing now.

I wish I could tell you exactly how I feel, but I don't even know myself. The truth is, I am very confused about this whole thing. I need some time to think about it, but I just don't have any.

I have a confession to make. I tried to figure out who you were. I don't know why I thought that would make a difference. Anyway, I've found out that's impossible, so I guess it really is up to us. I was a little frightened before about finding out who you were. Now, I'm terrified. It feels like so much depends on this one letter. Should I reveal myself or not?

I definitely think it's a good idea to write every day this week. I need more letters to figure all this out. I'll tell you one thing for sure. I promise that if you decide in your next letter to tell me who you are, I will tell you who I am, and then we can meet and go on from there. Who knows? Everything might turn out all right and surprise us both. I don't mean to sound off-the-wall. You mean a lot to me. No matter what happens, I'll always have warm feelings for you.

Your loving friend,
GHS

Chapter Twelve

"Hey, what happened? You missed study hall," Theresa said as she walked over to our lockers, where I was waiting for her.

"Oh, I got held up in computer class," I replied.

She laughed a little. "You're such a whiz in there. Why were you stuck, extra credit or something?"

"Nothing like that. I just had to talk to Miss McIntyre about something. You know, Theresa, she is really a wonderful person."

"Yeah," Theresa agreed, opening her locker. "She's very nice."

"She really cares about her students," I went on. "I wish all the teachers here were like her."

"Yeah, so do I," Theresa answered as she threw her books inside the locker. "Actually, when you think about it, most of the teachers here are pretty good. I mean, we haven't really got anybody truly terrible."

"Yup, you're right," I agreed.

"Except maybe Miss Kerr. But she isn't really awful, just boring, and I guess that isn't her fault." Theresa noticed I wasn't really listening to her. "What's wrong?" she asked again.

"Oh, nothing," I lied, still thinking about STX's last letter.

"Come on, Katie," Theresa prodded. "Bobby is going to the dance with you. You should be really excited, and you're not. What's the matter?"

"I got another letter from STX." Theresa slammed her locker, and we started walking down the hall to the lunchroom.

"So, what did it say?"

I took a deep breath and spilled the whole thing out. I finished the story, even what I wrote to STX, and Theresa and I went in to the lunchroom and got in line. I bought a salad and some iced tea, which I drink winter and summer. Theresa picked up some awful pizza, and we sat down.

"So, what do you think?" I asked her.

"I think you did just the right thing." She took a bite of the pizza. "Wow, this stuff is awful!"

"I know it is. Why do you keep getting it?"

"I always hope it'll get better." She set the pizza down and took a swallow of my iced tea, "But back to your romance problem. It isn't like you've got to decide to marry one or the other."

"That's true."

Theresa took another bite of the pizza. "Yuck!"

"Theresa, stop doing that! You're making me sick."

She took another sip of my tea.

"Theresa, do you want me to get you something to drink?"

"No, this'll be fine." She put her mouth back on the straw and looked up at me with her eyes crossed. That really cracked me up, and we both started to laugh.

Suddenly Theresa stopped laughing. I looked up and saw Tammy sliding into the seat next to mine. "I just talked to Bobby, and he tells me you asked him to the Varsity Prom," she said angrily. "Is that true?"

I was pretty scared, but I forced myself to sound calm. "Yes, it's true, Tammy. Why?"

She really blew up at that. "Why? Because it's just about the sleaziest thing I've ever heard of! You know that Bobby and I are going together!"

"*Were* going together," Theresa said to her.

She whirled on Theresa. "You keep out of this!"

Theresa started to wind up, but I stopped her. "It's OK, Theresa." I turned back to Tammy. "So, what's the problem?"

"The problem is, you are doing your best to break us up!"

"Bobby has never said anything to me about you. If you two are such a hot item, how come he said he'd go to the dance with me?"

She took a deep breath. "Bobby's too nice. That's *his* problem, and sometimes it's *my* problem, too. Like right now. Look, Katie, Bobby thinks you're a nice person and all. He probably just felt sorry for you when he said he'd go with you."

I couldn't believe she was sitting there, feeding me all those lies and expecting me to believe them.

She went on. "It looks like they're going to elect me queen of the court, and I want Bobby for my king. It would be awful if I had the wrong date."

"Oh, my heart breaks for you," Theresa said sarcastically.

"Look, I told you—"

I stepped in quickly. "It's OK, Theresa." I

turned to Tammy. "Listen, I'm sorry if all this hasn't worked out the way you planned, Tammy. If you and Bobby have an arrangement, I suggest you work it out and have him tell me about it. Otherwise, please leave me alone."

"Bobby isn't going to do that. He feels obligated to take you because he said he would. It's up to you to break the date."

"Up to me?"

"That's right. That is, if you have any sense of decency."

"Amazing," Theresa muttered under her breath.

"Look, Tammy, if Bobby wants to break off our date, he can, and there'll be no hard feelings," I said maturely. "Now, I wish you'd just leave me alone so I can finish my lunch."

Tammy was quiet for a second. Then she started talking in a very low voice. "I don't think I've made myself clear—"

"You have made yourself perfectly clear," I yelled. Normally I never raise my voice, but I just couldn't take it anymore. "Now, I'm telling you just once more. Leave me alone!"

She sat there for just a second, trying to salvage some of her dignity. That was hard to do since everybody in the lunchroom was staring at us.

"You know, Katie," she said, standing up, "I really feel sorry for you. It's so sad when someone fools herself like this. If you need someone to talk to when your little dream breaks up, you can come to me." She started to walk away.

"Thank you, Tammy," I called after her. "If tragedy strikes, I'm sure you'll be the first to know." I sat there for a while looking at the remains of my salad. I didn't feel much like eating anymore.

Theresa reached across the table and grabbed my hand. "Hey, Katie, you know what she said was a lot of garbage."

I jumped up from the table. "Theresa, take my tray up for me, will you? I've got to run."

"Katie—"

"I'm all right," I told her, "I've just got to talk to someone." I smiled at her, and she smiled back. Theresa is terrific that way. She knows when she can be of help and when she should let me work things out myself.

I walked out of the lunchroom and over to the football field where I knew I'd find Bobby. He had gym class that period. I needed to find out his side of the story.

I knew there wasn't anything to all that junk Tammy had said, but I had to straighten things out once and for all. I was just going to lay the whole thing out for him. If he said he'd rather go to the prom with Tammy, that was fine. Well, sort of. But either way, I just had to know.

I walked out of the school and onto the field. I didn't even stop to get my coat. The class was just finishing up by running laps and stretching out. Bobby was talking to coach Steeby, who was the teacher, and with Ted Dunn and some other guys. All of a sudden I thought it was a really stupid idea to go out there like that. Just as I was thinking about turning around and going back in, Ted turned around and saw me. "Hey, Katie," he called.

I was stuck. Bobby turned around and saw me. "Hello," he called out brightly. He was in a stained sweat shirt and pants. He looked wonderful.

The coach looked at me and smiled. "Well, is that Katie McNamara?"

"Yes, it is, sir."

"Did you come to join our class?"

I laughed. "No, I don't think so."

He smiled. "Well, I'll tell you, if you're half the athlete your father was, I'd have you in here in a minute."

All the guys laughed.

Then the coach said, "That's it for today."

"Hey," I said to Bobby, "could I talk to you?"

"What's up?" he asked, walking over to me.

"Bobby, I don't know how to ask this, so I'm just going to come right out with it. Is there anything still going on between you and Tammy Sawyer?"

He looked surprised for a moment, then composed himself. "Why?" he asked.

"Well," I said, "if there is, I don't think it's right for you and me to go to the dance together."

He became very quiet and still, and I wished I'd never brought the subject up. There I was doing exactly what Tammy had wanted me to do, in a way. Finally Bobby said, "Has she been talking to you?"

"Uh-huh," I said, nodding. "But it's no big deal if you don't want to go with me."

He looked at me, a strange mixture of emotions playing across his face. "Do you want me to go with you?" he asked.

"Well, sure. I wouldn't have asked you if I didn't want you to."

"Well, I wouldn't have said yes if I didn't want to."

"Bobby, are you sure?"

"Of course I'm sure." He got a little mad then. "I can't imagine what she said to you."

"It was nothing, really." We started walking

down the field without saying a word. But Bobby was still upset, I could tell. "Look, I don't want you to have to worry about this. It's just a dance. Why don't we call the whole thing off?" He didn't say anything, so I kept on talking. "I thought it would be fun to go together, but maybe it was a bad idea. I don't want to cause any problems for you. What do you think?"

He stopped walking suddenly and turned to face me. "Aren't you cold out here without a coat?"

It kind of took me by surprise. "No, I'm not. Well, a little, maybe."

"Look, Katie. I really would like to go to the dance with you, but—"

But. I could see it coming. "That's OK. I understand."

"No, no, no, you don't understand. I was going to say, if you feel funny about it because of something Tammy told you and you've changed your mind, I don't want you to think you *have* to take me."

"I guess it depends on this," I said. "Is there still something between you two?"

He sighed and ran his hand through his hair. "There is something going on, but it isn't what you think."

"What does that mean?" I asked.

"It means, I want to go to the dance with you, OK?"

"You're sure?" I needed to hear it again.

"I'm sure," he said, smiling.

"OK." I nodded my head. "I'm glad we're going."

"Me, too," he said as he turned around and looked at the field. It was empty now except for us. "I guess I'd better go change."

"OK."

We looked at each other for a second. Then he put his hand on my shoulders. Slowly he pulled me close to him and bent his head down. He kissed me as naturally as if we'd done it a hundred times before. I think I'll always remember every detail about that kiss, the way his mouth felt, soft and warm, and the sound of the traffic just outside the playing field.

After what seemed like a very long time, he broke the kiss and pulled his head back slightly so that his lips rested on my forehead. We stood still for a second, then he backed up and smiled at me. "I didn't plan for that to happen," he said.

"I know," I answered.

"I'd better go now. See you later?"

"OK," I answered. He waved at me shyly and ran ahead of me into the school.

I stood there for a long time before the cold got to me and I went back in.

Chapter Thirteen

You might think that all my problems with Bobby were pretty much cleared up at that point. But that couldn't be further from the truth. After our talk, I felt even more mixed up if that's possible. Bobby still hadn't told me what was really going on between Tammy and him. For all I knew, it could still be going hot and heavy. His words kept running through my mind, "There is something going on, but it isn't what you think." What had he meant by that?

Then he had to go and kiss me, which only confused me more. True, it was awfully nice. But if anything was still going on between Tammy and him, what was he doing kissing me?

The letter I got in Miss McIntyre's class the next day didn't help make things any clearer in my mind.

STX1150 to GHS5915

Dear Friend,

Obviously this whole thing is getting a little complicated. You mentioned that things were going well with you and your other person. I'm glad for you. It seems like that's what you really want. The truth is, things are going surprisingly well for me, too. Everything isn't perfect, but I'm pretty happy with the way things are developing between my other person and me.

But now we have to figure out what to do about you and me. I've been thinking a lot about this lately and here is what I think. First of all, you mean so much to me. The things we have shared in this short time will always be very special to me. I will treasure them always.

But maybe we should leave our relationship the way it is. I'm worried about what might happen if we let in all the things that go along with being friends. Our friendship might get even more complicated than it is now. Can you understand that? I think someday you will. If I could tell you everything about myself, you would understand now, but I can't without betraying a trust. Keeping a promise means a great deal to me, and I have told someone I'd never talk about certain things.

I hope you aren't angry with me. We have time for three more letters, and I am looking forward to them. You will always be very special to me.

STX

Suddenly I felt the whole world closing in on me. For the first time, I realized what it would mean to lose STX. I didn't even think about what I was going to say, I just started to type.

GHS5915 to STX1150

Dear STX,

Look, I can't let it end like this. I remember everything we've said to each other about this, and I know that you're probably right not to reveal who you are. But when I think about not being able to talk to you, I feel like I'm losing my best friend. And that's exactly what's happening. So I am going to tell you who I am.

My name is Katie McNamara. I live at 357 North Abbington Street, and my phone number is 555-1663. I'm a junior, and I have short brown hair and brownish-green eyes. So now you have my address and phone number. If you don't feel like telling me who you are, you can still write to me or call me. Honestly, I just want to be able to talk to you every once in a while.

Well, the big mystery is over. Now you can do whatever you want. I'll be waiting to hear from you.

Your loving friend,
Katie

Quickly I sent the letter into the computer before I had a chance to change my mind. But I knew I was doing the right thing. I wanted STX to know who I was. I would worry about the consequences later.

The next day I rushed into class to get my reply. I punched in my code, but nothing appeared on the screen. I tried a few more times, but there was no letter. When I realized that, I began to feel conflicting emotions. It should have been the most exciting week of my life. The end of term coming up, and I was going to the Varsity Prom with Bobby. But I was feeling terribly sad.

I had said hardly ten words to Bobby since the day he'd kissed me. It was as though he got embarrassed whenever he saw me. He didn't seem unhappy, just quiet and shy, as if he didn't know what to say to me.

Then there was this thing with STX. I felt really betrayed. I had had the nerve to tell him my name and everything, and he didn't even have the courtesy to acknowledge my letter. It just showed me how wrong I could be about a person. I was really hurt. I had thought that STX was honest and wonderful, and there he was, throwing my gift of friendship away.

Well, fine. If that's the way he wanted it, that's the way he was going to get it.

GHS5915 to STX1150

Listen, I know we decided we wouldn't tell each other our names, and I know I broke my promise by telling you mine, but I don't care. I gave you total friendship, and you turned it down. Well, you haven't got the right to do that. It isn't fair for you to choose to be silent. We've shared too much already for that. Do you really want to throw it all away now?

Please, STX, I need you. If you ever felt anything for me, then at least answer me one more time. You don't have to tell me who you are, just tell me our relationship isn't completely over. You can't just end it like this. I won't let you. Answer me. Please, answer me.

GHS

Chapter Fourteen

"Hold still, Katie. How do you expect me to fasten your dress when you're fidgeting like that?" It was the night of the dance, and my mom was helping me with the final touches.

To look at me you would have thought everything was wonderful. I was wearing a new, black silk evening dress. It had long sleeves and a straight skirt, so it fit sleekly around my legs. It had a slit up one side and a very low-cut back; it was the most beautiful dress I had ever worn. To set it off, I'd added gold beads and matching earrings.

But, inside, I was a wreck. I wasn't looking forward to this evening at all. I was certain that

Bobby was going with me out of some sense of obligation. We'd probably have a terrible time because he'd be wishing I was somebody else.

STX had never answered my last letter. I called in on the machine every day, but there was nothing. Well, so much for honesty. I had talked the whole thing out with both my mother and Theresa, but it didn't really help. Both of them thought I had done the right thing with STX, but that didn't make me feel any better.

"Now, let me look at you," Mom said. She studied my reflection in the mirror. "Funny, you don't look like a girl who's going to a dance."

"I'm sorry, Mom. This must not be much fun for you."

"It's not supposed to be fun for me. It's supposed to be fun for you."

"Well, isn't it supposed to be really exciting, getting your daughter ready for a big dance and all?"

She laughed and sat down next to me at my vanity table. "Katie, if I have learned anything it is to never to expect things to work out the way other people tell you they're supposed to." She hugged me and rested her head against mine. I gave her a weak smile, then broke out into a full grin. "There, that's my girl," Mom said.

"I don't know why it all has to be so complex," I said, frowning again.

Mom smiled a little sadly. "When you were very little, maybe five or six years old, you used to call peanut butter and jelly sandwiches peanutjellybutters. Well, one day, it was one of the first times you were allowed to go out and play by yourself, you started to play with some of the other kids on the block. Most of them were older than you were. Well, when I called you in for lunch, you yelled, 'Oh boy, peanutjellybutters,' and all the other kids laughed at you. You stopped smiling, and you looked at them, and then you looked at me. I felt so sad. It was the first time I realized I couldn't always keep everything perfect and beautiful for you."

She looked very wistful for a moment, and I felt as if I should be cheering her up. I gave her a big hug and a kiss, and I stood up and twirled around for her. "So, how do I look?"

She smiled at me. "You are, at this moment, the most beautiful sixteen-year-old I have ever seen." We looked at each other for a moment, and then she stood up. "I'd better get downstairs and check on your father. He wants to take some pictures of you and Bobby, but as you know, he can't figure out that camera of his." She gave me another little kiss and walked out.

I checked myself over once more in the mirror, and I made a decision. I wasn't going to worry anymore. Not about Bobby, not about STX. I was going to put all that stuff out of my mind and have a good time. I nodded to myself in the mirror once. "That's the right idea," I said. "In a hundred years who's going to care?"

But my whole facade of strength crumbled into little pieces when the doorbell rang. I had to hold back the urge to bite my nails to bits.

Then Mom came to my room and knocked at the door. "Katie, honey, Bobby is here." She came in and smiled at me. "You set?"

"I guess so. I hope he didn't bring a corsage," I muttered. "They're so hard to pin on, and sometimes they ruin the look of a dress."

"Don't worry," Mom said. She gave me a little smile of support, and we went downstairs.

Bobby was in the den with my dad. They were talking football, of course. I could hear Bobby's voice. "Yeah, but he's got a lot of good freshmen coming up. I don't think he has anything to worry about."

As we walked into the room, Bobby was sitting with his back to the door, so it was Dad who saw me first. "Here she is."

Bobby stood up and turned around. He looked wonderful. He was wearing a beautiful black tuxedo with a vest and a wing-collared shirt and stylish black tie. He looked a little like Robert Redford at his best. I just about melted. "Hi," he said.

"Hi."

He held a long box out to me. "I didn't get you a corsage because I wasn't sure what color you were wearing, and anyway, I'm not wild about corsages. Do you mind?"

I gave him a big smile. "No, it's fine." I opened the box. In it were a dozen, long-stemmed white roses. They looked like old ivory. "They're beautiful," I said.

Dad jumped up and picked up his camera. "OK, I know you're both in a hurry to run off, but you have to indulge me with some pictures for a second."

"Oh, Dad."

"Come on, Katie, just one. It will only be a second." Then he spent about half an hour getting us in just the perfect position in front of the fireplace so we'd look natural and relaxed. He took about a dozen pictures. The flash didn't work for half of them, of course. It seemed like an hour before Bobby and I got out of the house and into the car.

"I'm sorry about all that."

He laughed. "Oh, it's OK. I like your folks."

"Thanks."

He turned to me and smiled. "You look very beautiful tonight."

"So do you," I said. I thought he was going to kiss me again, but he just put the car back into gear, and we backed out of the driveway. At first, I was a little disappointed, but then I remembered my decision to enjoy myself, and I just relaxed in Bobby's wonderful company.

I knew everything was going to be all right. Bobby and I were so relaxed and comfortable with each other. It was as if we'd done this a hundred times before.

We went to a wonderfully romantic restaurant on the other side of town for dinner. We both had lobster, which I could eat every day of my life and never get tired of. The restaurant was owned by some friends of Bobby's parents, so they kept coming over and making a big fuss over us. The piano player even dedicated a song to me. It was wonderful. I felt as if I were in a movie.

Bobby was very funny over dinner. I can't remember when I've laughed so hard. I mean, a lobster can be a little hard to eat at first because it's just lying there on the plate looking at you. But Bobby started talking to his like it was an old friend, and then he would lean down and listen as if it were whispering to him. It was a riot.

After the lobster we had some incredibly delicious chocolate mousse.

As we sat drinking our tea, I felt very quiet, and I think Bobby did, too. We didn't say anything for a while. We'd just look up every once in a while and stare at each other. Then we'd both break into big, happy grins. Bobby finally said, "You know, I was really nervous about tonight."

"You were?"

"Yeah. Were you?"

"You bet," I said with a laugh. He was quiet again. I could tell he wanted to say something, but he didn't know how to start. I touched his hand. "What are you thinking?"

"Oh, nothing."

"Come on."

He smiled. "I was just—well—I'll tell you later." I didn't push him. Everything was so relaxed, and I was having too good a time.

We left the restaurant, and Bobby bought me a clown puppet from a little store that was still open, "Oh, it is so cute," I said.

"What are you going to name him?"

I thought about it for a second. "Peanutjellybutter," I said.

Bobby laughed. "A weird choice." Then we walked to the car and drove to the dance.

The gym was really crowded when we arrived. The band was playing a Police song, and everyone was dancing. The decorations looked wonderful. Multicolored streamers and balloons hung from the ceiling. There was a big trellis with crepe paper leaves and flowers all over it, which was being used as a backdrop for photographs. A long table draped in white cloth held the punch bowl and snacks.

Several of our friends yelled to us as we walked in. Theresa and Alan came over immediately. She looked terrific in a long, simple, rose-colored dress. She steered me tactfully away from Alan and Bobby so we could talk. "How's it going?" she asked me. "You look great."

"Thanks, so do you," I said. "It's going really beautifully. Dinner was wonderful."

Suddenly she wrapped her arms around me and gave me a big hug. "I'm so happy for you, Katie. I just knew it would work out."

I hugged her back. "Thanks. It's going to be a great evening."

She let go of me and smiled. "I know it is."

Alan and Bobby came over to us, and Alan started to pull Theresa to the dance floor. "Hey," he said, "come on. Music waits for no man or woman." Theresa laughed, and they spun out onto the floor.

"How about joining the action?" Bobby asked me.

"Sure," I said.

I've always loved dancing, but never so much as with Bobby. We must have danced about ten songs right in a row. Bobby's a terrific dancer, and that night he was really going wild.

When the band took a break, Miss McIntyre, a chaperon, went up to the mike. She thanked everyone who had worked on the committees, and some of them came up and took bows. Bobby and I stood and listened, his arm around my shoulder, mine around his waist.

It felt so right being there with him like that. Miss McIntyre continued. "We'll announce the prom court before the band comes back on. In the meantime we'll play some records so you can keep on dancing."

As music blasted out over the sound system, I turned to Bobby and said, "Let's take a break. I want to get something to drink."

"I'll get it for you," he offered. "The line's pretty long."

"Thanks," I said.

Bobby started off, but Ted Dunn stopped him. "Hey, Bobby, can I talk to you for a second?"

Bobby turned to me and gave me a little helpless shrug. "That's OK," I said. "I'll get it. Do you want anything?"

"No, just hurry back." I smiled at him and took off for the refreshment table.

Pat Powers was there filling glasses. "Great dance, huh?" he asked.

"The best," I said.

He smiled at me as he handed me a glass of punch. "You and Bobby look really terrific together out there."

"Thanks, Pat."

He looked down for a minute. Then he glanced up and caught my eye. "Katie, can I talk to you for a second?"

"Sure."

He seemed strangely embarrassed. "It's about the computer class," he finally blurted out.

"I knew it! I knew I was right all along. I just had a feeling it was you, Pat. Why didn't you tell me sooner?"

He looked a little surprised. "You know?"

"Yes, I know."

"I'm sorry. I should have asked you earlier, but I thought you might be too busy."

"Too busy? What are you talking about?"

He gave me a funny look. "I thought you knew. I'm not doing too well in my computer class sixth period, and Miss McIntyre said you might be willing to help me study for the final."

"Oh."

"What's wrong, Katie? You look sort of disappointed."

I smiled at him. "It's nothing, Pat. Sure. Sure, I'd be glad to help."

He smiled his thanks, and I finished my drink. A slow, melancholy song was playing over the sound system, and all of a sudden I felt I had to be with Bobby. I wanted to look into his eyes, to have him hold me in his arms.

I rushed back to where he had been talking to Ted, but he wasn't there. I scanned the dance floor, but I couldn't find him. I figured he must have gone over to the refreshment table to meet me. Then, as I turned around to go back, I spotted him with Tammy. They were dancing together to the soft, sweet music. He was smiling into her eyes.

Everything sort of blurred after that. I walked out of the gym and into the empty hall. All I knew was that I had to get out of there. Away from Bobby, away from Tammy.

The halls were deserted and quiet. I could hear only an echo of the music and voices from the gym. The happy sounds floating down the hall mocked me. My tears came hot and fast. The last thing I wanted was to bump into somebody I knew. So I ran into the first open classroom I came to. I didn't even bother to shut the door.

Oddly enough, it was the computer room. It was always quiet in there, but now it was even more so. There was only the sound of my own sobbing. Gradually my tears subsided. I sat down at one of the desks and stared at the TV screen. I could just make out my reflection, distorted in the curved glass.

So, it was true. It was all true. Bobby would have rather been with Tammy all along. He was probably telling her that right now. Maybe he was saying he was sorry he'd had to go with me to the dance, but she knew how it was. He had given his word, and he couldn't go back on it, not without hurting old Katie's feelings. *Don't worry,* I imagined him saying, *I'll get rid of her quickly, and then I'll stop over at your house later.* Then they'd laugh, and he'd kiss her. After that, maybe he'd remember me and go off to find me. Only I wouldn't be there. Not now. Not ever again.

So, the worst that could happen had happened. I had lost Bobby, whom I never really had had in the first place, and I had lost STX, whom I had never really known. I hurt more than I had ever hurt in my whole life.

If only the term weren't over. If only I could still write STX and tell him how I was feeling. I wished I had his advice now. He'd always helped me figure out just how things were supposed to be. But now I'd never talk to him again.

I slapped the keyboard in frustration, and several letters appeared on the screen. The computer was on! Miss McIntyre must have forgotten to turn it off.

Well, I decided, there was going to be one last letter. One last letter to STX, which he would never read, and then I was kissing both him and Bobby Allen goodbye.

I made a lot of mistakes on that letter, but here's what I typed.

GHS5915 to STX1150

You really let me down. I thought you were my friend, but you let me down. Maybe I expected too much from you, but I think you could have at least answered my letter.

I can say just about anything I want in this letter because I know you'll never read it. I guess that's how it should have been all along. We tried to make it that way, but we didn't succeed completely. I would have been able to say that I thought you were beautiful. I was trusting you to be beautiful always, but I know now that isn't possible. Not for you or for anyone. Even me, I guess.

There is something else that brought this on; it isn't all you. My other person let me down, too. I don't know if he was just trying to be kind to me or what, but it turns out he isn't the person I thought he was, either. So here I am, caught in the middle.

Both of you have hurt me more than anyone else could, but it's really not your fault. It's mine, for expecting too much. I wanted more than you could give, and I got hurt. Well, at least I learned something from it. I learned I can never trust anyone that much again. It just makes me too easy a target. There's no sense in my writing any more. I'm going home.

I didn't sign it. I don't know why, I guess part of it was because I didn't see much reason to, and part of it was that I started crying really hard after I sent the letter into the computer. The letter went off line by line. It was like watching pieces of me being torn away.

I don't know how long I sat that way. What brought me out of it was my computer beeping. I brought my head up and watched as a message typed itself across the screen.

STX1150 to GHS5915

Dear Katie,

You're right that you expect too much. I think you expect the world to be as beautiful as you are. I, for one, have never seen anything else as beautiful, unless it is a frozen lake in winter or the first flowers of spring. Don't blame yourself. It isn't your fault.

All my love,
STX1150

I looked up slowly. There was Bobby, sitting at a terminal across the room. We stared at each other for a long time before either of us spoke. "It was you. It was you all the time," I said, the truth dawning on me.

He smiled at me. "I didn't know how to tell you. I almost came out with it at dinner, but something held me back. I don't know why, I was afraid you'd be—disappointed."

"Disappointed?" I couldn't believe my ears.

"Yes," he said and nodded. He stood up and moved a little closer to me.

I wiped my eyes. "But what about Tammy?"

"I couldn't tell you this until it was all resolved, but it is now. I—it's hard to begin. You know I was involved with her, but I realized it was for all the wrong reasons. It was hard to do, but I finally broke it off with her. But Tammy wouldn't accept that. She was sure I was just going through a phase. Then we had a long talk, and I confided in her how I felt about you. That was before I knew how you felt about me. After I told her, it just made her more insistent about us getting back together. That's when she started talking to you. I guess she wasn't very nice to you."

"You can say that again," I told him.

"She wanted to keep us apart. That was why she called at the Christmas party. You know, I wanted to explain to you then about Tammy and me, and I really wanted to tell you how I felt about you. But it wasn't that simple because I was also thinking about GHS the way you were thinking about STX. I didn't have any idea it was you on the other end of those wonderful letters. I should have guessed, but I didn't."

"Neither did I," I said, smiling.

"Anyway, that night when I went over to

Tammy's, we had it all out. She's not a very good loser. She was so upset, but, you see, I couldn't just leave her cold. I was trying to make her understand that we just weren't right for each other. She couldn't see that—until tonight, when she saw you and me together."

"But why didn't you tell me you were STX when you found out I was GHS?" I wanted to know.

"I should have," Bobby said. "I was going to do it tonight. But I wanted it to be perfect. Then Tammy came up and asked me for that dance, just for old times' sake. That was when she told me she finally understood about you and me. She's not happy about it, but she finally accepts it. I saw you too late, and it took me until now to find you. If I'd been using my head, I would've looked here first thing." He glanced down at his feet for a second, then lifted his head and stared straight into my eyes. "I hope you can forgive me."

I sat there stunned for a second. My mind was in a whirl, but I knew exactly what I was doing. I walked across to him. He stood up, and we looked into each other's eyes for a moment before I wrapped my arms around his neck and felt his lips on mine. I don't know how long that kiss lasted. It felt as if it went on forever. Finally we broke apart.

Bobby smiled down at me and looked around the computer lab. "This is sort of a weird place for romance. Don't you think?"

I smiled back. "Well, you know what they say."

"What?" he whispered.

"We live in a computer age." I laughed.

He laughed with me and then bent down to kiss me again. "Well," he said. "I guess this means that everything has worked out pretty well."

I looked into those beautiful eyes of his. I nodded my head slowly and smiled at him. "Shup," I said.

A LETTER TO THE READER

Dear Friend,

Ever since I created the series, SWEET VALLEY HIGH, I've been thinking about a love trilogy, a miniseries revolving around one very special girl, a character similar in some ways to Jessica Wakefield, but even more devastating—more beautiful, more charming, and much more devious.

Her name is Caitlin Ryan, and with her long black hair, her magnificent blue eyes and ivory complexion, she's the most popular girl at the exclusive boarding school she attends in Virginia. On the surface her life seems perfect. She has it all: great wealth, talent, intelligence, and the dazzle to charm every boy in the school. But deep inside there's a secret need that haunts her life.

Caitlin's mother died in childbirth, and her father abandoned her immediately after she was born. At least that's the lie she has been told by her enormously rich grandmother, the cold and powerful matriarch who has raised Caitlin and given her everything money can buy. But not love.

Caitlin dances from boy to boy, never staying long, often breaking hearts, yet she's so sparkling and delightful that everyone forgives her. No one can resist her.

No one that is, but Jed Michaels. He's the new boy in school—tall, wonderfully handsome, and very, very nice. And Caitlin means to have him.

But somehow the old tricks don't work; she can't

seem to manipulate him. Impossible! There has never been anyone that the beautiful and terrible Caitlin couldn't have. And now she wants Jed Michaels—no matter who gets hurt or what she has to do to get him.

So many of you follow my SWEET VALLEY HIGH series that I know you'll find it fascinating to read what happens when love comes into the life of this spoiled and selfish beauty—the indomitable Caitlin Ryan.

Thanks for being there, and keep reading,

Francine Pascal

A special preview of the exciting
opening chapter of the first book
in the fabulous new trilogy:

CAITLIN

BOOK ONE

LOVING

by Francine Pascal,
creator of the best-selling
SWEET VALLEY HIGH series

"That's not a bad idea, Tenny," Caitlin said as she reached for a book from her locker. "Actually, it's pretty good."

"You really like it?" Tenny Sears hung on every word the beautiful Caitlin Ryan said. It was the petite freshman's dream to be accepted into the elite group the tall, dark-haired junior led at Highgate Academy. She was ready to do anything to belong.

Caitlin looked around and noticed the group of five girls who had begun to walk their way, and she lowered her voice conspiratorially. "Let me think it over, and I'll get back to you later. Meanwhile let's just keep it between us, okay?"

"Absolutely." Tenny struggled to keep her excitement down to a whisper. The most important girl in the whole school liked her idea. "Cross my heart," she promised. "I won't breathe a word to anyone."

Tenny would have loved to continue the conversation, but at just that moment Caitlin remembered she'd left her gold pen in French class. Tenny was only too happy to race to fetch it.

The minute the younger girl was out of sight, Caitlin gathered the other girls around her.

"Hey, you guys, I just had a great idea for this year's benefit night. Want to hear it?"

Of course they wanted to hear what she had to say about the benefit, the profits of which would go to the scholarship fund for miners' children. Everyone was always interested in anything Caitlin Ryan had to say. She waited until all eyes were on her, then hesitated for an instant, increasing the dramatic impact of her words.

"How about a male beauty contest?"

"A what?" Morgan Conway exclaimed.

"A male beauty contest," Caitlin answered, completely unruffled. "With all the guys dressing up in crazy outfits. It'd be a sellout!"

Most of the girls looked at Caitlin as if she'd suddenly gone crazy, but Dorothy Raite, a sleek, blond newcomer to Highgate, stepped closer to Caitlin's locker. "I think it's a great idea!"

"Thanks, Dorothy," Caitlin said, smiling modestly.

"I don't know." Morgan was doubtful. "How are you going to get the guys to go along with this? I can't quite picture Roger Wake parading around on stage in a swimsuit."

"He'll be the first contestant to sign up when I get done talking to him." Caitlin's tone was slyly smug.

"And all the other guys?"

"They'll follow along." Caitlin placed the last of her books in her knapsack, zipped it shut, then gracefully slung it over her shoulder. "Everybody who's anybody in this school will just shrivel up and die if they can't be part of it. Believe me, I wouldn't let the student council down. After all, I've got my new presidency to live up to."

Morgan frowned. "I suppose." She took a chocolate bar out of her brown leather shoulder bag and began to unwrap it.

Just at that moment, Tenny came back, empty-handed and full of apologies. "Sorry, Caitlin, I asked all over, but nobody's seen it."

"That's okay. I think I left it in my room, anyway."

"Did you lose something?" Kim Verdi asked, but Caitlin dismissed the subject, saying it wasn't important.

For an instant Tenny was confused until Dorothy Raite asked her if she'd heard Caitlin's fabulous new idea for a male beauty contest. Then everything fell into place. Caitlin had sent her away in order to take credit for the idea.

It didn't even take three seconds for Tenny to make up her mind about what to do. "Sounds terrific," she said. Tenny Sears was determined to belong to this group, no matter what.

Dorothy leaned over and whispered to Caitlin. "Speaking of beauties, look who's walking over here."

Casually Caitlin glanced up at the approaching Highgate soccer star. Roger Wake's handsome face broke into a smile when he saw her. Caitlin knew he was interested in her, and up until then she'd offhandedly played with that interest—when she was in the mood.

"And look who's with him!" Dorothy's elbow nearly poked a hole in Caitlin's ribs. "Jed Michaels. Oh, my God, I've been absolutely dying to meet this guy."

Caitlin nodded, her eyes narrowing. She'd been anxious to meet Jed, too, but she didn't tell Dorothy that. Ever since his arrival as a transfer student at Highgate, Caitlin had been studying him, waiting for precisely the right moment to be introduced and to make an unforgettable impression on him. It seemed that the opportunity had just been handed to her.

"Hey, Caitlin. How're you doing?" Roger called out, completely ignoring the other girls in the group.

"Great, Roger. How about you?" Caitlin's smile couldn't have been wider. "Thought you'd be on the soccer field by now."

"I'm on my way. The coach pushed back practice half an hour today, anyway. Speaking of which, I don't remember seeing you at the last scrimmage." There was a hint of teasing in his voice.

Caitlin looked puzzled and touched her fingertips to her lips. "I was there, I'm sure—"

"We were late, Caitlin, remember?" Tenny spoke up eagerly. "I was with you at drama club, and it ran over."

"Now, how could I have forgotten? You see,

Roger"—Caitlin sent him a sly, laughing look—"we never let the team down. Jenny should know—she's one of your biggest fans."

"Tenny," the girl corrected meekly. But she was glowing from having been singled out for attention by Caitlin.

"Oh, right, Tenny. Sorry, but I'm really bad with names sometimes." Caitlin smiled at the girl with seeming sincerity, but her attention returned quickly to the two boys standing nearby.

"Caitlin," Dorothy burst in, "do you want to tell him—"

"Shhh," Caitlin put her finger to her lips. "Not yet. We haven't made all our plans."

"Tell me what?" Roger asked eagerly.

"Oh, just a little idea we have for the council fund-raiser, but it's too soon to talk about it."

"Come on." Roger was becoming intrigued. "You're not being fair, Caitlin."

She paused. "Well, since you're our star soccer player, I can tell you it's going to be the hottest happening at Highgate this fall."

"Oh, yeah? What, a party?"

"No."

"A concert?"

She shook her head, her black-lashed, blue eyes twinkling. "I'm not going to stand here and play Twenty Questions with you, Roger. But when we decide to make our plans public, you'll be the first to know. I promise."

"Guess I'll have to settle for that."

"Anyway, Roger, I promise not to let any of this other stuff interfere with my supporting the team from now on."

At her look, Roger seemed ready to melt into his Nikes.

Just at that moment Jed Michaels stepped forward. It was a casual move on his part, as though he were just leaning in a little more closely to hear the conversation. His gaze rested on Caitlin.

Although she'd deliberately given the impression of being impervious to Jed, Caitlin was acutely aware of every move he made. She'd studied him enough from a distance to know that she liked what she saw.

Six feet tall, with broad shoulders and a trim body used to exercise, Jed Michaels was the type of boy made for a girl like Caitlin. He had wavy, light brown hair, ruggedly even features, and an endearing, crooked smile. Dressed casually in a striped cotton shirt, tight cords, and western boots, Jed didn't look like the typical preppy Highgate student, and Caitlin had the feeling it was a deliberate choice. He looked like his own person.

Caitlin had been impressed before, but now that she saw him close at hand, she felt electrified. For that brief instant when his incredible green eyes had looked directly into hers, she'd felt a tingle go up her spine.

Suddenly realizing the need for an introduction, Roger put his hand on Jed's shoulder. "By the way, do you girls know Jed Michaels? He just transferred here from Montana. We've already got him signed up for the soccer team."

Immediately the girls called out a chorus of enthusiastic greetings, which Jed acknowledged with a friendly smile and a nod of his head. "Nice to meet you." Dorothy's call had been the loudest, and Jed's gaze went toward the pretty blonde.

Dorothy smiled at him warmly, and Jed grinned back. But before another word could be spoken, Caitlin riveted Jed with her most magnetic look.

"I've seen you in the halls, Jed, and hoped you'd been made welcome." The intense fire of her deep blue eyes emphasized her words.

He looked from Dorothy to Caitlin. "Sure have."

"And how do you like Highgate?" Caitlin pressed on quickly, keeping the attention on herself.

"So far, so good." His voice was deep and soft and just slightly tinged with a western drawl.

"I'm glad." The enticing smile never left Caitlin's lips. "What school did you transfer from?"

"A small one back in Montana. You wouldn't have heard of it."

"Way out in cattle country?"

His eyes glimmered. "You've been to Montana?"

"Once. Years ago with my grandmother. It's really beautiful. All those mountains . . ."

"Yeah. Our ranch borders the Rockies."

"Ranch, huh? I'll bet you ride, then."

"Before I could walk."

"Then you'll have to try the riding here—eastern style. It's really fantastic! We're known for our hunt country in this part of Virginia."

"I'd like to try it."

"Come out with me sometime, and I'll show you the trails. I ride almost every afternoon." Caitlin drew her fingers through her long, black hair, pulling it away from her face in a way she knew was becoming, yet which seemed terribly innocent.

"Sounds like something I'd enjoy,"—Jed said, smiling—"once I get settled in."

"We're not going to give him much time for riding," Roger interrupted. "Not until after soccer season, anyway. The coach already has him singled out as first-string forward."

"We're glad you're on the team," Caitlin said. "With Roger as captain, we're going to have a great season." Caitlin glanced at Roger, who seemed flattered by her praise. Then through slightly lowered lashes, she looked directly back at Jed. "But I know it will be even better now."

Jed only smiled. "Hope I can live up to that."

Roger turned to Jed. "We've got to go."

"Fine." Jed nodded.

Caitlin noticed Dorothy, who had been silent during Jed and Caitlin's conversation. She was now staring at Jed wistfully as he and Roger headed toward the door.

Caitlin quickly leaned over to whisper, "Dorothy, did you notice the way Roger was looking at you?"

Her attention instantly diverted, Dorothy looked away from Jed to look at Caitlin. "Me?" She sounded surprised.

"Yeah. He really seems interested."

"Oh, I don't think so." Despite her attraction to Jed, Dorothy seemed flattered. "He's hardly ever looked at me before."

"You were standing behind me and probably couldn't notice, but take my word for it."

Dorothy glanced at the star soccer player's retreating back. Her expression was doubtful, but for the moment she'd forgotten her pursuit of Jed, and Caitlin took that opportunity to focus her own attention on the new boy from Montana. She knew she only had a moment more to make that unforgettable impression on him before the two boys were gone. Quickly she walked forward. Her voice was light but loud enough to carry to the girls behind her.

"We were just going in your direction, anyway," she called. "Why don't we walk along just to show you what strong supporters of the team we are?"

Looking surprised, Roger said, "That's fine by us. Right, Jed?"

"Whatever you say."

Caitlin thought he sounded pleased by the attention. Quickly, before the other girls joined them, she stepped between the two boys. Roger immediately tried to pull her hand close to his side. She wanted to swat him off, but instead, gave his hand a squeeze, then let go. She was pleased when Diana fell in step beside Roger. Turning to Jed, Caitlin smiled and said, "There must be a thousand questions you still have about the school and the area. Have you been to Virginia before?"

"A few times. I've seen a little of the countryside."

"And you like it?"

As they walked out the door of the building, Jed turned his head so that he could look down into her upturned face and nodded. There was a bright twinkle in his eyes.

Caitlin took that twinkle as encouragement, and her own eyes grew brighter. "So much goes on around here at this time of year. Has anyone told you about the fall dance this weekend?"

"I think Matt Jenks did. I'm rooming with him."

"It'll be great—a real good band," Caitlin cooed. In the background she heard the sound of the others' voices, but they didn't matter. Jed Michaels was listening to *her*.

They walked together for only another minute, down the brick footpath that connected the classroom buildings to the rest of the elegant campus. Caitlin told him all she could about the upcoming dance, stopping short of asking him to be her date. She wasn't going to throw herself at him. She wouldn't have to, anyway. She knew it would be only a matter of time before he would be hers.

It didn't take them long to reach the turnoff for the soccer field. "I guess this is where I get off," she said lightly. "See you around."

"See you soon," he answered and left.

Caitlin smiled to herself. This handsome boy from Montana wasn't going to be an easy mark, but this was an adequate beginning. She wanted him—and what Caitlin wanted, Caitlin got.

"You going back to the dorm, Caitlin?" Morgan asked.

"Yeah, I've got a ton of reading to do for English lit." Caitlin spoke easily, but her thoughts were on the smile Jed Michaels had given her just before he'd left.

"Somerson really piled it on tonight, didn't she?" Gloria Parks muttered.

"Who cares about homework," Caitlin replied. "I want to hear what you guys think of Jed."

"Not bad at all." Tenny giggled.

"We ought to be asking *you*, Caitlin," Morgan added. "You got all his attention."

Caitlin brought her thoughts back to the present and laughed. "Did I? I hadn't even noticed," she said coyly.

"At least Roger's got some competition now," Jessica Stark, a usually quiet redhead, remarked. "He was really getting *unbearable*."

"There's probably a lot more to Roger than meets the eye," Dorothy said in his defense.

"I agree. Roger's not bad. And what do you expect," Caitlin added, "when all he hears is how he's the school star."

The girls started crossing the lawns from the grouping of Highgate classroom buildings toward the dorms. The magnificent grounds of the exclusive boarding school were spread out around them. The ivy-covered walls of the original school building had changed little in the two hundred years since it had been constructed as the manor house for a prosperous plantation. A sweeping carpet of lawn had replaced the tilled fields of the past; and the smaller buildings had been converted into dormitories and staff quarters. The horse stable had been expanded, and several structures had been added—classroom buildings, a gymnasium complete with an indoor pool, tennis and racketball courts—but the architecture of the new buildings blended in well with that of the old.

"Caitlin, isn't that your grandmother's car in the visitors' parking lot?" Morgan pointed toward the graveled parking area off the oak-shaded main drive. A sleek, silver Mercedes sports coupe was gleaming in the sunlight there.

"So it is." Caitlin frowned momentarily. "Wonder what she's doing here? I must have left something at the house last time I was home for the weekend."

"My dream car!" Gloria exclaimed, holding one hand up to adjust her glasses. "I've told Daddy he absolutely *must* buy me one for my sixteenth birthday."

"And what did he say?" Jessica asked.

Gloria made a face. "That I had to settle for his three-year-old Datsun or get a bicycle."

"Beats walking," Morgan said, reaching into her bag for another candy bar.

"But I'm dying to have a car like your grandmother's."

"It's not bad." Caitlin glanced up at the car. "She has the Bentley, too, but this is the car she uses when she wants to drive herself instead of being chauffeured."

"Think she'll let you bring it here for your senior year?"

Caitlin shrugged and mimicked her grandmother's cultured tones. " 'It's not wise to spoil one.' Besides, I've always preferred Jaguars."

Caitlin paused on the brick path, and the other girls stopped beside her. "You know, I really should go say hello to my grandmother. She's probably waiting for me." She turned quickly to the others. "We've got to have a meeting for this fundraiser. How about tonight—my room, at seven?"

"Sure."

"Great."

"Darn, I've got to study for an exam tomorrow," Jessica grumbled, "but let me know what you decide."

"Me, too," Kim commented. "I was on the courts all afternoon yesterday practicing for Sunday's tennis tournament and really got behind with my studying."

"Okay, we'll fill you guys in, but make sure you come to the next meeting. And I don't want any excuses. If you miss the meeting, you're out!" Caitlin stressed firmly. "I'll catch the rest of you later, then."

All the girls walked away except Dorothy, who lingered behind. Just then, a tall, elegantly dressed, silver-haired woman walked briskly down the stairs from the administrative office in the main school building. She moved directly toward the Mercedes, quickly opened the driver's door, and slid in behind the wheel.

Caitlin's arm shot up in greeting, but Regina Ryan

never glanced her way. Instead, she started the engine and immediately swung out of the parking area and down the curving drive.

For an instant Caitlin stopped in her tracks. Then with a wide, carefree smile, she turned back to Dorothy and laughed. "I just remembered. She called last night and said she was dropping off my allowance money but would be in a hurry and couldn't stay. My memory really *is* bad. I'll run over and pick it up now."

As Caitlin turned, Dorothy lightly grabbed Caitlin's elbow and spoke softly. "I know you're in a hurry, but can I talk to you for a second, Caitlin? Did you mean what you said about Roger? Was he really looking at me?"

"I told you he was," Caitlin said impatiently, anxious to get Dorothy out of the picture. "Would I lie to you?"

"Oh, no. It's just that when I went over to talk to him, he didn't seem that interested. He was more interested in listening to what you and Jed were saying."

"Roger's just nosy."

"Well, I wondered. You know, I haven't had any dates since I transferred—"

"Dorothy! You're worried about dates? Are you crazy?" Caitlin grinned broadly. "And as far as Roger goes, wait and see. Believe me." She gave a breezy wave. "I've got to go."

"Yeah, okay. And, thanks, Caitlin."

"Anytime."

Without a backward glance, Caitlin walked quickly to the administration office. The story about her allowance had been a fabrication. Regina Ryan had given Caitlin more than enough spending money when she'd been home two weeks earlier, but it would be all over campus in a minute if the girls thought there was anything marring Caitlin's seemingly perfect life.

Running up the steps and across the main marble-floored lobby that had once been the elegant entrance hall of the plantation house, she walked quickly into the dean's office and smiled warmly at Mrs. Forbes, the dean's secretary.

"Hi, Mrs. Forbes."

"Hello, Caitlin. Can I help you?"

"I came to pick up the message my grandmother just left."

"Message?" Mrs. Forbes frowned.

"Yes." Caitlin continued to look cheerful. "I just saw her leaving and figured she was in a hurry and left a message for me here."

"No, she just met on some school board business briefly with Dean Fleming."

"She didn't leave anything for me?"

"I can check with the part-time girl if you like."

"Thanks." Caitlin's smile had faded, but she waited as Mrs. Forbes stepped into a small room at the rear.

She returned in a second, shaking her head. "Sorry, Caitlin."

Caitlin forced herself to smile. "No problem, Mrs. Forbes. It wasn't important, anyway. She'll probably be on the phone with me ten times tonight."

As Caitlin hurried from the main building and set out again toward the dorm, her beautiful face was grim. Why was she always trying to fool herself? She knew there was no chance her grandmother would call just to say hello. But nobody would ever know that: She would make certain of it. Not Mrs. Forbes, or any of the kids; not even her roommate, Ginny. Not anyone!

Like it so far? Want to read more? LOVING will be available in May 1985.* It will be on sale wherever Bantam paperbacks are sold. The other two books in the trilogy, LOVE DENIED and TRUE LOVE, will also be published in 1985.

*Outside the United States and Canada, books will be available approximately three months later. Check with your local bookseller for further details.

We hope you enjoyed reading this book. All the titles currently available in the Sweet Dreams series are listed on the next two pages. They are all available at your local bookshop or newsagent, though should you find any difficulty in obtaining the books you would like, you can order direct from the publisher, at the address below. Also, if you would like to know more about the series, or would simply like to tell us what you think of the series, write to:

Kim Prior,
Sweet Dreams,
Transworld Publishers Limited,
61–63 Uxbridge Road,
Ealing, London W5 5SA.

To order books, please list the title(s) you would like, and send together with your name and address, and a cheque or postal order made payable to TRANSWORLD PUBLISHERS LIMITED. Please allow cost of book(s) plus 20p for the first book and 10p for each additional book for postage and packing.

(The above applies to readers in the UK and Ireland only.)

If you live in Australia or New Zealand, and would like more information about the series, please write to:

Sally Porter,
Sweet Dreams,
Corgi & Bantam Books,
26 Harley Crescent,
Condell Park,
N.S.W. 2200,
AUSTRALIA.

Kiri Martin,
Sweet Dreams,
c/o Corgi & Bantam Books New Zealand,
Cnr. Moselle and Waipareira Avenues,
Henderson,
Auckland,
NEW ZEALAND.